"Do you really think I've come three thousand miles to look at buildings and bridges?"

"I . . . I don't know," she said, then added inconsequentially, "I've read somewhere that when good Americans die they go to Paris."

"But I'm alive, Mollie, and not all that good. Can you deny that there's been something between us from the very beginning? Why are you fighting me?" he whispered, his voice seductive in the soft night air.

He looked at her carefully, then caught his breath sharply. Once again he lowered his face to hers slowly. This time she was ready for him. He kissed her gently at first, then more insistently, and as his strong arms enfolded her she forgot her reservations and responded eagerly, matching his hunger with her own, molding her body to his. "Fire at last," she thought she heard him whisper before all thought ended . . .

Dear Reader:

After more than one year of publication, SECOND CHANCE AT LOVE has a lot to celebrate. Not only has it become firmly established as a major line of paperback romances, but response from our readers also continues to be warm and enthusiastic. Your letters keep pouring in—and we love receiving them. We're getting to know you—your likes and dislikes—and want to assure you that your contribution does make a difference.

As we work hard to offer you better and better SECOND CHANCE AT LOVE romances, we're especially gratified to hear that you, the reader, are rating us higher and higher. After all, our success depends on *you*. We're pleased that you enjoy our books and that you appreciate the extra effort our writers and staff put into them. Thanks for spreading the good word about SECOND CHANCE AT LOVE and for giving us your loyal support. Please keep your suggestions and comments coming!

With warm wishes,

Ellen Edwards

Ellen Edwards
SECOND CHANCE AT LOVE
The Berkley/Jove Publishing Group
200 Madison Avenue
New York, NY 10016

SURPRISE ENDING
ELINOR STANTON

SECOND CHANCE AT LOVE
BOOK

SURPRISE ENDING

First edition published August 1982

First printing

"Second Chance at Love" and the butterfly emblem are trademarks be-
longing to Jove Publications, Inc.

Printed in the United States of America

Second Chance at Love books are published by
The Berkley/Jove Publishing Group
200 Madison Avenue, New York, NY 10016

To J. J.,
who made the real Mollie bloom
—E. S.

The heart has its reasons, which reason
doesn't know.

—Blaise Pascal, *Pensées*

- 1 -

REALLY, AT TWENTY-NINE she should have known better than to let him come in for a nightcap, Mollie thought. And because she had weakened under his persistent pleading, here she was at two in the morning darting around her new pale gray velour sofa and trying to convince this persistent Romeo that she meant it when she said she wasn't interested in having him spend the night—not even on that same living room sofa.

"Why not?" Larry Lambert asked petulantly.

Mollie Paine looked thoughtfully at the slender young man in the tight-fitting designer jeans. Fighting back her growing exasperation, she said as mildly as she could, "Oh, Larry, please don't sulk. It's just that it would be such a shame to ruin an evening that's had its—" she groped for a polite formula "—its own special fascination by allowing a possible misunderstanding—"

He didn't let her finish. "Unsure of yourself?" he asked, tossing back his golden ringlets with a studied gesture that had probably served him well in the past.

Mollie's blue-gray eyes flashed with warning. "Don't force me to be cruel, Larry. In all the years I've been living in New York I've found many things to be unsure of, but frankly, my ability to resist your special charms doesn't rate high among them."

She stopped abruptly, aware that she was losing her temper and becoming shrill, then went on in what she

1

hoped was a gentler tone. After all, she couldn't afford
to offend the boy genius from San Francisco! "Look, my
friend, you're a talented poet whose books add luster to
the Lorne publishing list. And I'll grant that you also
have a certain charm..." That was a mistake, she realized immediately, and took a precautionary step back
to compensate for a step forward by Larry. "However,"
she went on hurriedly as she sought refuge behind a small
end table, "you are really little more than a boy
and—"

"Mollie! I'm twenty-four!"

"That's just it. You're..." She gasped as his words
finally penetrated. "You're *twenty-four?* Are you sure?"

"Of course I'm sure! Why are you so surprised?"

How could Mollie possibly explain that all evening
long she had felt as if she were with an adolescent? *I
want...come on...let's go...I'm bored....* He wasn't
seeing New York with her, Mollie, but with a "sophisticated young editor I'd like to make out with." Still, she
couldn't very well say that; her boss would never forgive
her if Larry Lambert took his book of new poems elsewhere.

So she mumbled something about his boundless energy.

"That's not what you mean," he said with unexpected
shrewdness. "You're not that much older than I am—at
least you don't look it. Twenty-six?" he guessed, his
eyes seeming to go right through her apricot-colored silk
blouse and chocolate-brown velvet skirt in a rapid re-
connaissance of the body underneath. "Besides, nobody
cares about that kind of thing these days, so don't try to
sound so mature and wise in the ways of the world."

Not wise at all, she reflected as she watched Larry
warily across the length of the gray and rose carpet, or
I wouldn't be in this situation. Damn Jim Lorne! Three
years ago, when he had interviewed her for the job as
associate editor, she'd told him she was a *working* editor,

never happier than when her blue pencil was speeding through the pages of an overfat manuscript that needed slenderizing. She told him she loathed the social side of the New York publishing world, with its business lunches and "important" cocktail parties. And that she was essentially one of those benighted people who thought her time, except for the occasional emergency, was her own after five—or at most six—o'clock.

And Jim Lorne had nodded understandingly, insisted that that was just what he was looking for, given her a decent salary, a windowed office, more and more responsibility—and also somehow wheedled her into being the unofficial hostess for the firm. Every time one of his male authors breezed into town, she was maneuvered into showing him around the Big Apple. Too often the tour turned out to be a tussle.

She had on several occasions found herself wondering what there was about New York air that lowered the erotic boiling point of all these visiting literati. But at least the older ones could usually be brought back into line at an awkward moment with an innocent request to see a picture of the wife and kiddies incautiously mentioned earlier in the evening. The younger ones were more difficult—Larry being one of the *most* difficult. As the petted poet of America's youth, he wasn't used to rejection. He had not only the manners but also the morals of a goat, and he was positively famished for the experience of an affair with what he evidently considered both an "Eastern intellectual" and a tantalizing "older woman."

Well, she was damned if she was going to be anybody's "New York Experience"!

"Mollie, don't you like men?"

"I beg your pardon?"

"You looked angry. And since I can't be all that hard to take"—he smiled slyly—"I just wondered if it's men in general . . ."

I really don't need this, Mollie thought with another quick glance at her watch, managing to do it without ever taking her eyes completely off him. "Larry, you've been reading too many of the wrong kind of books. I like men quite well, and someday I even hope to have one of my own. A *real* one. Now be a good *boy* and go away. It's two-eighteen in the morning," she said with a precision that she hoped would have the effect of a cold shower on him.

"Just my point," he wheedled, ignoring the underlying message. "You know how dangerous New York streets can be in the middle of the night. You wouldn't want to turn me out and then have my blood on your conscience, would you?"

"You'll be at least as safe here in the East Sixties as you would be in Haight-Ashbury back in San Francisco," she snapped. But the conviction had gone out of her voice. It *was* late for a weekday night, and he didn't know anything about the city except its discos. . . . "Okay, Larry," she said, resigned, "you win."

His eyes gleamed and she added hastily, "You can sleep on the couch. You'll find a blanket, a pillow, and some men's pajamas in the hall closet."

"Ye gods! You girls are too much! You make all this fuss and then it turns out you keep a spare pair of men's pajamas handy." He was laughing now. Triumphant. "I won't need them. I sleep in the raw, and my love usually keeps me warm."

"Suit yourself, Narcissus. This *woman* is turning in for what's left of the night."

Fully aware that he was close on her heels, she moved quickly toward her bedroom door as she spoke. On the threshold she turned abruptly. "As for the pajamas, think what you will." She felt the usual pang at the thought of those pajamas—Tim's pajamas, and a bittersweet memento—and, with her hand on the knob, smiled as she added, "Just remember that I'm not a clause in your contract with Lorne Publications."

With one swift movement she entered her room, closed the door, and pulled the bolt. After four years in the small but charming one-bedroom apartment she had been lucky enough to find after she and Tim were divorced, Mollie had more than once been grateful for what she had originally thought an extraordinary cautiousness displayed by the previous tenant—a lock on one's own bedroom door.

On the other side of the door, she heard Larry exclaim in exasperation, "Mollie, that's not fair! Don't you trust me?"

Her lips against the door, she purred as sweetly as possible, "Of course I do. But why put an unnecessary strain on your sense of honor?"

"Mollie!"

"Good night, Larry. And by the way—they say that love laughs at locksmiths, but that was probably in a less technically sophisticated age."

After a long pause she heard him mutter, "You New York women are something else!"

At least she had taught him the difference between women and girls . . .

Mollie could hear him opening the hall closet. A moment later he was back outside her door. "Whose monogram is this?" he asked. *"T.D.?"*

Hesitating a second, Mollie answered wearily, "Just someone I used to know." Or thought I did, she added to herself as she undressed quickly, got into her nightgown and robe, and walked slowly over to the old oak rolltop desk that just fit between the two windows. Pensively she ran her hand over its scarred surface, wondering just why she had kept only this of all the furniture that she and Tim had bought in the early days of their marriage. They had both fallen in love with Victoriana, and their only quarrels had been about whether to buy one chair or another.

The desk certainly didn't go with any of her other furniture, she mused, looking around as if seeing the room for the first time. Instead of curlicues and furbelows, there were soothing straight lines. Victoriana had never really been her thing, she had soon realized. It was just another example of how she had allowed herself to sacrifice her own personality on the altar of domestic peace. She knew better now. But when a marriage breaks up, one is entitled to a little sentimentality, and with her that sentimentality had taken the form of a desk and a pair of pajamas—the last birthday gift she had bought for Tim and never had a chance to give him...

Shaking her head as if to clear away old memories, Mollie looked at the pile of paper on the desk—the Roger Herrick manuscript. It was proving so troublesome—my God, what a low opinion of women that man had!—that she had broken her own rule and brought it home to work on. Chapter Four was staring her in the face, but she realized that 2:30 in the morning was no time to match wits with such an author, so she sighed, turned away from the desk, and went to bed, thinking of some of the problems posed by the manuscript. I'll sleep on it, she told herself—an expression that generally meant she'd spend the night tossing and turning. But this time she was asleep the moment her head hit the pillow.

The next thing she knew the alarm clock and her telephone were simultaneously fighting for her attention. Lifting what she thought was the phone, she found herself staring into an illuminated digital announcement of the time—seven o'clock. She groaned, and as she tried to replace the clock on the night table, it crashed to the floor. The phone was still ringing.

"You can come out from behind the barricades. You're safe now—I'm at Kennedy."

"Larry!" She sat bolt upright in bed, completely

awake. "Where did you say you were?"

"Kennedy."

"What are you doing there? We're supposed to have a meeting tomorrow—I mean today—with Jim Lorne about your new collection of poems."

"I'm not sure I'm going to give them to Lorne," he said airily.

"But it was all settled yesterday!" She could barely control her indignation. "Larry, you're the closest thing I know to an old-fashioned cad—and so young, too." Mollie slammed the receiver down, hoping she had at least dented his intolerable ego with that last observation. But his ego was probably as impervious as his brain.

Mollie always enjoyed her walk from the bus stop at Twentieth Street and Second Avenue to her office, no matter what the season. It was mid-April now, but there was no hint of spring in the damp air, and Gramercy Park still looked bare and colorless. Soon, soon, she told herself...

A few minutes later she was sitting in her office, staring unseeingly past the row of plants on the windowsill and trying to think of how to tell Jim Lorne that because of her unwillingness to "play the game"—a phrase she hated—she had lost one of his most promising money-makers, a young lyric "genius" whose poems were currently being set to music by half the rock groups in America.

Biting her lip, she automatically began to open her morning mail. The first letter was from a midwestern professor who announced the arrival—under separate cover and heavily insured—of a novel on which he had labored for seven years. Not surprisingly, it concerned a midwestern professor who had everything to make him happy, but..."Good Lord, another saga of male menopause," she moaned.

"What was that, honey?" Betty, the receptionist-file

clerk-den mother, was standing in the doorway, looking more matronly than modish in her blue nylon pantsuit.

"I said another saga of male menopause is being offered to Lorne Publications."

"Male menopause?" Betty was genuinely puzzled. "I didn't know that—"

"Never mind, Betty. Forget it," Mollie snapped.

Betty looked hurt.

"Sorry, Betty," Mollie apologized, "but it's been a rough morning after a rougher night."

"You poor dear," Betty said in a soothing tone. "And I'm afraid your troubles aren't over yet. Mr. Lorne just stormed in and he wants to see you immediately."

He's probably already heard from Larry Lambert, Mollie thought unhappily. Nevertheless, as she reached for the container of black coffee she had brought with her in a brown paper bag, and she said firmly, "Tell the Ayatollah that I refuse to discuss anything until I've had my morning fix."

"He sounds mad, honey. Maybe you'd better not wait."

Once again Mollie was amazed at how people of Betty's generation snapped to when the master's voice growled out a command. After twenty years with the company, she should have learned that Jim Lorne's bark was meant to disguise a complete absence of bite—especially since he knew damn well that if Betty left nobody would ever be able to find any of the letters and contracts she had filed under a system all her own.

"Well, much madness is divinest sense, I'm told," Mollie said flippantly. "In any case, he has only himself to blame."

"Blame for what?"

"For trying to turn me into a call girl."

To avoid having to explain her comment to Betty, Mollie took a sip of coffee and reached again for the pile of mail.

"I'll tell him you're in the Ladies," said Betty after a pause. "Don't worry, honey. You'll feel better when you've had your coffee."

"Don't you dare tell him I'm in anything called the *Ladies!*" Mollie cried out after Betty's retreating back. "Tell him exactly what I said."

"Don't worry, I'll handle it," Betty replied over her shoulder.

"I'll bet," mumbled Mollie, resolutely returning to her mail.

A square-shaped mauve envelope caught her eye. Curious, she slit it open and extracted a matching piece of notepaper that immediately filled the office with the sickeningly heavy scent of heliotrope. Her eyes dropped rapidly to the signature at the bottom.

Of course! Who else would have such awful taste? Last year Jim had sent her to Paris to visit the editorial offices of a few of the important French publishers. While she was there, she indulged herself one evening by spending the price of a dress on a meal at the famous Grand Véfour restaurant. If she closed her eyes, Mollie could still conjure up every delicious mouthful of that dinner— and see, at the table alongside hers, the incredible vision of purple ruffles topped by an extravagantly plumed lilac hat. The lady, for such the heliotrope-scented mass turned out to be, had been badgering the almost despairing waiter about her food.

"C'est vraiment affreux!" she had shouted, turning to Mollie for support.

"Oh no, my meal's been delicious—not awful at all," Mollie had answered, sipping the Grand Marnier liqueur she had ordered with her coffee.

"American, no?" The plumed hat lifted sufficiently to allow its owner's button-bright eyes to take in Mollie. "But in that case you're in no position to judge, my child. Such culinary innocents, you Americans." Her tone was one of scientific detachment.

Odette Gerard—for that was the lady's name—turned out to be friendly but opinionated—in other words, Mollie decided, very French. She had graduated from the celebrated Cordon Bleu cooking school, she had explained, and *la cuisine* was her *grande passion*.

Dring.

Mollie reluctantly left her memories of that unusual night in Paris and turned to the black phone squatting on her desk.

"Mollie?"

"Good morning, Jim." She hesitated, then plunged right ahead. "I suppose you've heard that I've been had?"

"By whom?"

"Larry Lambert," she confessed.

Jim was silent at the other end of the line, then said in a languid voice, "I didn't know women of your caliber smiled on fools like Lambert. However, given his importance to the firm, I suppose that's better than laughing at him outright."

Mollie snorted. "You idiot! I'm talking about the contract for his new collection of poems."

"Oh, that," Lorne replied. Mollie had expected an angry outburst, but Jim seemed quite unconcerned about the man who got away. "Don't give it another thought. We've got bigger fish to fry this morning. Roger Herrick's in from Chicago and on his way here in a rage about something you've done to the first three chapters of his new novel, *A Woman in Love.*"

"Done? What with last week's escort duty and Larry last night, I hardly had time to do a thing to it. I only tried to qualify some of his more outrageous comments about female psychology."

"I guess that's why he's furious. He said something about not wanting any frustrated schoolmarm playing around with his masculine prose."

"It's not his masculine prose but his masculine pose I find so hard to take." She took a deep breath. "Jim, why don't you give this book to one of the other editors? Peter could probably do a good job on it."

Once again there was a silence at the other end of the wire while Mollie held her breath and waited. She was gambling. She didn't want to give up working on the book, but she had to have the authority to handle Herrick as she thought best. And given her vision of him—a middle-aged curmudgeon whose notions of female behavior seemed inspired by observations made in his hometown's stockyards—she would need every bit of authority she could muster.

Jim's answer surprised her. "Was Larry that bad? I've never heard you talk like this before." He paused. "Are you really asking to be taken off what will probably be the big novel of the year?"

Mollie exploded. "Listen here, Jim Lorne, I've had a hell of a night because of you. Instead of me showing Larry Lambert around, I've been lugged to every rock joint in the Village, Soho, So-Soho, Noho, Tribeca, and points north, east, south, and west! I've had to listen to his immortal lyrics sung by vocal groups who should have been drowned in their infancy—or at least had their adenoids removed—"

"Hush, child. Don't fuss about Larry—or the contract. Naturally I insisted that he sign with us before I would let him go out with you. Today's problem is Roger Herrick, fresh from Chicago and the triumphs of his last masterpiece—*The Weaker Sex*. I'd . . ."

She hardly heard the last few words, because as soon as she had registered what he was saying about the Lambert contract Mollie slammed down the receiver. Bolting up from her seat, she stormed toward Jim's office. A few words had transformed her from a sorely tried, somewhat apologetic young woman into a fire-breathing dragon. The indistinct sounds now issuing from her throat were actually an amalgam of unladylike words fused together by the heat of her anger.

Rushing past Betty's desk in the mahogany-paneled central hallway that separated the two wings of the ground-floor offices, Mollie was vaguely aware that the receptionist was talking to someone. She had a fleeting impression—tall, dark, deep-voiced—but she was too upset to pay any real attention.

"Mollie, this gen—"

"Not now, Betty."

"But, Mollie..."

By the time that sentence must have ended, Mollie was already flinging Jim's door open. "That's the last time you pull something like that on me, James Aloysius Lorne! Has it ever occurred to you that even a mere woman might have some sense of dignity? Has it ever..."

Her voice faltered as she was faced by the sight of the imperturbable Jim Lorne, who looked up and calmly set down the cup of coffee Betty had freshly brewed for him that morning, as she did every morning. Not for this scion of old New York the usual brown-bag routine. At least not so long as there were Bettys in the world to wait on him, Mollie noted scornfully.

"It's customary to knock. There's also a little nicety known as saying good morning. Good morning, Mollie...or rather, Miss Paine, since you seem so unfriendly."

Never had her surname struck her as being so apt. Pain! That's what she was—all blistering pain and humiliation. But this was the last time, positively the last time she would let this monster use her as a lure, a decoy—or, as with Larry, a reward.

Still unruffled, Jim once more took up his cup. "And now that that little lesson in etiquette is over, in what way may I serve you?" He bent his head slightly, took an exploratory sip from his cup. "Damn that woman! I've told her a million times—only one sugar." He looked to Mollie as though for sympathy.

At the sight of this 250-pound, immaculately dressed, pink and white Humpty Dumpty sitting there with his pinky extended genteelly, Mollie's anger dissolved into laughter. "Oh, what's the use?" she wailed, sinking into the chair in front of his desk.

"None at all, my dear." He looked at her benignly and continued his lecture. "You've just given a remarkable demonstration of the instability of the female temperament. I can't think how you ladies expect to survive—much less thrive—in the rough and tumble of the editorial business."

"I manage very well," she shot back, "in the editorial business, as you darn well know. It's the monkey business I can't cope with."

"Actually, you're not doing all that well editorially either. As I was saying on the phone, that overeager blue pencil of yours has managed to infuriate the most valuable editorial property in our stable."

"Damn Roger Herrick! He's a genius of sorts, I suppose," Mollie acknowledged grudgingly, "but from the first few chapters of his *A Woman in Love* I would say he's never met a woman who wasn't either a jellyfish or a piranha."

A slight cough sounded from the doorway. "I'm afraid I've come at an inopportune moment, but your receptionist said I'd find Miss Paine here."

Though spoken mildly, the words echoed in the suddenly silent room. Mollie, whose back was toward the door, watched Jim nervously shuffle a pile of papers, and she knew without a doubt that the low, resonant voice belonged to the man she had glimpsed talking to Betty—and that both voice and body belonged to Roger Herrick. Rising slowly, she turned to face him, standing defiantly as straight as she could, determined not to back down.

She caught her breath, then hurriedly tried to mask her surprise. This was not at all the man she had imagined, yet as soon as she saw him she felt he could never be anyone other than who he was. This man *had* to be Roger Herrick, and Roger Herrick had to look exactly like this man. How could she have been so wrong? Middle-aged curmudgeon indeed!

He stood at the threshold of the room, a somewhat tousled head of thick, dark hair, curling at the ends; dark brows slightly raised over piercing black eyes that immediately met and held hers; sharply defined lips upturned in barely restrained amusement; and a strong jaw that bespoke determination and even obstinacy. There was something almost sculptural about the sharp planes of his face with its strongly carved features; and his tall, lean, but powerful frame exuded an air of total ease and control, a sense of strength and forcefulness—leashed for the moment, but unmistakably present, to be drawn upon when needed.

"It would be pointless to pretend that I didn't overhear your last remark," he said, his intelligent eyes now appraising her carefully. "Miss Paine, I presume?"

"Yes, I'm Mollie Paine," she replied, sounding too defensive even to her own ears but resolved not to let him see how he unsettled her. He was probably in his mid-to-late-thirties, she decided, trying to match his dispassionate examination with her own, and to say that he was handsome would somehow misrepresent him. *Handsome* was a word for some of the boy-men she had known in college; for Tim, with whom she had allowed herself to become, finally, foolishly infatuated; or for many of the young men she met in her working world. It would do to describe Larry Lambert, for example— but it was decidedly inadequate for this man who was so sure of himself as he leaned casually against the door. Even the conventional gray flannel suit worn with a blue Oxford shirt and a discreet maroon tie couldn't camouflage his compelling physical presence.

The sound of a cup being rattled reminded her of Jim, and she forced herself to turn toward him.

"Mollie," he began, getting up from his chair with as much grace as his bulk would allow, "this is, as I'm sure you have gathered, Roger Herrick—do come in, Roger— whose new novel you seem to have misunderstood."

"On the contrary, Lorne. She may have understood it very well." When he turned to Mollie, his eyes were positively gleaming with mockery. "I'm afraid, Miss Paine, that you're absolutely right. I never *have* been fortunate enough to meet a woman whom love did not turn into what you so aptly describe as either a jellyfish or a piranha. My experience"—he emphasized the word slightly—"has led me to the conclusion that there are only two kinds of women—those who surrender their personalities along with their persons, or those who turn into savage shrews when confronted by love. The first is just as dangerous as the second, but a bit more difficult to spot." His jaw was hard and uncompromising, and in his fixed stare Mollie felt the unspoken question: and you—which kind are you?

With some effort Mollie recovered her self-control, pleased at the firmness with which she was able to speak. "I won't deny that I'm embarrassed to have been over-heard, Mr. Herrick, but perhaps it's all for the best. This way our editor-author relationship can begin in com-plete—if enforced—candor. Let me start by saying that I think you're an enormously talented writer, but that I loathed your last book and I don't see that your approach has changed very much."

"Mollie!" Jim gasped in horror.

"Oh, be quiet, Lorne, and let Miss Paine have her say. I know what *you* think—or rather I know you're prepared to approve of anything I write as long as my books keep selling. Miss Paine's point of view may be unflattering, but I'm sure it's offered in all honesty.

Please go on," he concluded, once more turning on her
the full force of his eyes, of such hypnotic fire that they
seemed to melt away her powers of both reason and
speech.

My God, could he be right? Were woman such rub-
bishy beings after all? For something deep within her
was about to cry uncle when she realized that the fire in
those eyes had no more warmth than the smoke from a
piece of dry ice. She stiffened immediately.

"Perhaps you wouldn't mind a preliminary question?"
she asked coolly.

He shrugged his shoulders and she couldn't decide if
he was expressing indifference or consent. After a brief
hesitation she chose to take it for the latter. "Have you
ever been in love?"

For a moment she thought she had gone too far, that
he was enraged, but he seemed to catch himself and
merely replied coldly, "Perhaps you had better define
what you mean by love, Miss Paine."

"You're stalling, Mr. Herrick. You know perfectly
well what I mean by love. Even those who have never
experienced it know what it is, what it should be."

"Wiser people than us have been badly hurt because
of their inability to recognize it." His tone was acerbic.

Before she could reply, he turned to Lorne and asked
brusquely, "What do *you* think, Lorne?"

"Oh, love," Jim answered, adjusting his bulk in his
chair and waving a pudgy hand dismissively. "I suspect
a man can have only one passion in his life, and mine
is for literature."

At this statement both Mollie and Herrick burst out
laughing. Herrick was the first to recover. "Come off it,
Lorne! Everybody knows that the only serious reading
you do is the monthly profit-and-loss statement. I'll bet
you haven't read anything since Cock Robin."

"That may be because nobody—including yourself,

Roger—has written anything quite that exciting for many years." Jim looked offended, and when Mollie turned to Herrick again, the glance that passed between them was one of perfect understanding.

"Come now, Mr. Herrick," she said, returning to the original charge, but in an atmosphere lightened by their laughter. "We were talking about love."

"Talking about it is seldom very satisfactory."

"Nevertheless, that's the item on the agenda of this impromptu editorial conference. And to save you any further embarrassment, I withdraw my question as overly personal. Let me instead tell you what I think a woman looks for in love."

"I deny that you embarrass me, but I'm all ears," he replied with a mocking bow.

"Try being a little heart as well," Mollie rejoined tartly. Before he could reply, she continued, "A woman is looking for a love relationship based not on submission or domination but on sharing and equality."

"You mean by sharing, I suppose, half a man's present income and a lien on his future earnings after the romance has run its course," he drawled.

Mollie was angry. Their brief truce was evidently over. "I can see that you're determined not to discuss this seriously. Don't you suppose I know what I'm talking about?" Memories of her refusal to take one cent of alimony from Tim made her tone more curt than she liked, but he seemed not to notice.

"I'm sure you think you do," he said courteously. "But I find that though women are seldom in doubt about the ideas they cling to, they *are* often in error."

"Who was it," said Mollie, turning to Jim Lorne, "who said that man was given speech so that he could hide his thoughts?" Without waiting for Jim to answer, she wheeled around and added impetuously, "Meeting you, Mr. Herrick, has been a . . ."

"Pleasure?" he asked, helpfully filling the pause.

"...an experience. And now I'll leave you and Mr. Lorne alone. You must have things to discuss."

She left the room without another look at either of them.

- 2 -

Mirror, mirror on the wall, who's the fairest one of all?

"Not you, my girl," Mollie murmured ruefully to her image in the women's room mirror. That hair! She lifted a lock, held it in the air a moment, and then, sighing deeply, let it fall back onto her head. It was a wonder the sight of her hadn't turned Roger Herrick to stone, she thought, reaching for her brush.

Her hand poised midway, she suddenly stopped in amazement. Was she really worried about what that man thought about her hair? My God—he had been so angry that he probably hadn't noticed *what* she looked like, and wouldn't have cared anyway. Why was she standing here brooding about it? Because she found him attractive, she admitted without a second's hesitation.

Stepping back from the mirror to get a full-length view, she tried to see what he had seen. The reflection showed a tall, slim young woman, a little pale from a long New York winter; good eyes, fringed with dark thick lashes; a generous mouth; gleaming hair, unruly now from the morning's damp air, but well-shaped and layered, cut to fall nicely into place with a minimum of care, its honey-gold color set off by a blue angora turtle-neck; a flannel A-line skirt which emphasized her small waist, the same blue-gray as her eyes. It all added up, she thought, abruptly tiring of her self-examination and leaving the ladies' room, to the fact that though more

19

than one man had told her otherwise, the figure in the mirror was certainly no beauty. It had never bothered her before, but now . . . Now she found herself wondering what conclusion Roger Herrick had drawn after scrutinizing her—and why it was so important to her.

She couldn't deny the intensity of her response to him. It had been months since she'd met a man who interested her at all, and she had *never* felt such an immediate and strong attraction to anyone as she did for Roger Herrick—not even to Tim, who had had to woo her for almost a year before she agreed to marry him. The men she had met recently—pudgy hedonists like Jim Lorne, adolescent cherubs like Larry Lambert, or the assortment of happily or unhappily married men looking for brief affairs—had convinced her she would probably never find another man she would want to spend the rest of her life with. But Roger Herrick was different from any man she had ever met, and she knew that his reactions to everything—including her—would be different too. What would it be like, she wondered, moony as an adolescent, to know him—talk to him, laugh with him, feel his arms around her, kiss him . . .

"That Herrick is sure some hunk of man," said Betty, unwittingly interrupting Mollie's daydream as she walked past the receptionist's desk.

Mollie forced herself back to reality. "Think so?" she replied noncommittally.

Betty was not a genius, she thought as she returned to her office and once more took up Odette's letter. But sometimes she put things in a way that got right to the point. Mollie had to admit that Roger Herrick was indeed "some hunk of man."

"Ma chère Mollie," the letter began. "You no doubt wonder why you have not heard from me. I don't write, but I think often of you.

"I have much good news. An old aunt who I never

see has died and left me *beaucoup d'argent*. Well máybe not a lot of money, but enough for me to start up the cooking school of my dreams. I'm going to use it to set up the Gerard Ecole de Cuisine, and I keep one place in my first class for you.

"Do not waste time and postage to thank me. Just take the *avion* to Paris immediately.

> I'm counting on you,
> Odette Gerard

The letter was dated the first of the month. As she put it down, Mollie smiled, remembering the meals she and Odette had shared after their first meeting at the Grand Véfour. Odette hadn't prepared them; despite her culinary diplomas and ambitions, when it came to dinners Odette was best at making reservations.

They had enjoyed an extraordinary gastronomic tour of Paris—at Mollie's expense, it was true, but the meals had never been very expensive. And they were always in places where tourists seldom set foot. Mollie would never forget Chartier's on rue Montmartre, a working-class restaurant where the food was only tolerable but the art nouveau decor was magnificent and the clients were like a bit of old France. She would never have discovered it on her own.

The Gerard Ecole de Cuisine, Mollie mused, might not be a *culinary* experience, but it was bound to be an experience of some kind. It sounded like fun, but she couldn't possibly take a trip now. The place Odette was saving for her would have to go to someone else. What a shame. April in Paris must be enchanting...

The phone rang.

"Mollie," said Jim in a voice heavy with sweetness, "Roger Herrick is on his way to your office. It's important that you be nice to him. You will, won't you?"

In spite of the fact that her heart had leaped joyously,

Mollie forced a coolness into her tone. "I'm nice to everybody, but why is it especially important that Herrick be cosseted? Look, Jim, my name is Mollie Paine, not Moll Flanders."

Jim's voice assumed a sharper edge. "You're to be nice to him because I ask you to. He's the biggest money-maker on our list, and if you need a more compelling reason, I'd like to remind you that it's the income from his last book that helped bail out some of those slim, sensitive novels you're so fond of acquiring."

A knock sounded on her open door and Mollie looked up to find the man in question standing there. Impelled by some wicked genie, she waved him to a chair in front of her desk and said into the phone, "No, Mr. Mailer, I really don't think so. Yes, I knew you'd understand. Yes, do that. I'll be looking forward to your call." An oily chortle from Jim Lorne, who had obviously understood that Herrick had arrived, oozed from the receiver into her ear. "You're learning," he said before she could hang up.

"Was that Norm?" Roger Herrick asked, folding himself easily into the chair she had indicated.

More than a hint of mockery tinged his voice and Mollie was suddenly ashamed. Here she was constantly calling for candor and honesty, yet allowing herself to be carried away into playing a cheap trick—and one that hadn't fooled him for a moment.

"I'm afraid," she said after a slight hesitation, "that what you have just witnessed was a brief audition by Mollie Paine girl actor for the role of Mollie Paine girl editor."

He looked mildly interested but said nothing, and Mollie realized he wasn't going to make it any easier for her. She forced herself to meet his eyes. "That was Jim Lorne warning me you were on the way and suggesting I be 'very nice' to you, since the income from your bestseller helped pay off the deficit from some 'sensitive' first novels I've talked him into doing."

"I see." His deep, rich voice was amused. "And now you're in a bind."

"What do you mean?" Mollie's surprise was genuine. She hadn't anticipated a problem beyond that of making her confession.

"I assume being very nice means—at least for starters—taking me out to an expense-account lunch?"

"Of course. But—oh, you mean . . ."

"Exactly, Miss Paine. I mean that you would, of course, like to . . . lunch . . . with me, but you don't care to do it on instructions from Jim Lorne. Am I correct?"

Yes, she would like to have lunch with him, but she couldn't bear to think it was so obvious. "Not exactly," she improvised. "The problem is more that if I'm not nice, I antagonize both you and my boss. But if I am nice, you know it's for ulterior motives—and that can hardly please a man like you, Mr. Herrick."

A quick flicker of surprise passed over his face. "Well done," he murmured appreciatively, then extended his right hand across Mollie's desk. "Perhaps we ought to begin all over again . . . Mollie."

"I'd like that . . . Roger," she replied, putting her hand into his. It nestled there, safe and warm in his firm grasp, and she withdrew it with a distinct feeling of regret. "Now what?"

"Now you will have lunch with me."

"How does that solve my problem?"

"Simple. *I'm* inviting *you*. It's out of your hands."

"I'm not free to refuse?"

"How would you explain that to all those starving young novelists whose fate depends on our working to-gether successfully? Besides, common courtesy demands that you be nice to a visitor to your city. I don't know many people here."

"Not even Norm?" she asked wickedly.

"I admire the man's books, but I know him about as well as you do." He grinned.

When he smiled he was irresistible. In a rush of romantic feeling that Mollie would have disavowed if she could, she fancied that the dingy gray light filtering through her window on this cheerless April day was banished by a ray of warm sunlight from an unknown source.

"But it's only eleven-thirty," she temporized, some part of her resisting the tumultuous feelings this man had aroused.

"Fine," he said easily. "That will give us time to have a leisurely drink and get to know each other before we talk seriously about the editing of *A Woman in Love.*"

"You still want me to do it? I thought you'd had enough of my schoolmarmish changes."

Roger Herrick's dark eyes flashed dangerously. "Jim ought not to tell tales out of school," he said curtly.

"Perhaps not," she agreed, rising and heading for the coat rack in the corner of the office. "But James Aloysius Lorne usually behaves as best suits his convenience."

She reached for her raincoat, but Roger was there before her and already holding it out for her. As he helped settle the coat on her shoulders, his hands deliberately lingered for a moment. She told herself not to panic. He couldn't possibly know what had happened to her at his touch. As a matter of fact, she would have been hard put herself to describe what had happened, what she had felt. . . . Her voice a bit unsteady, she said, "I think I'm quite ready for that drink and lunch."

Unhurriedly, as if well aware of what was passing through her mind, he said with mock gallantry, "Your wish is my command."

If only that were so, she thought, moving toward the door, her thoughts in a state of semiparalysis. She was astonished and more than a little shocked by some of the images flooding her imagination, and she avoided meeting his eyes.

Lorne Publications, a small but prestigious company, was not located in a midtown skyscraper of the kind that housed firms like Random House or Simon and Schuster, but in an equally small but prestigious brownstone off Gramercy Park, a bit of old New York that had miraculously escaped the speculator's bulldozer. As Roger and Mollie walked past the iron-railed private park, Mollie wondered how she had failed to notice earlier that the trees and shrubs inside had already taken on a hopeful haze of green. She sniffed the air tentatively.

"That's charming," said Roger.

"Yes, it is," she replied, thinking he was referring to one of the lovely old houses across the street, on the south side of the square. "That's the Player's Club. It used to be the home of the actor Edwin Booth."

But when she turned to him, she saw that he wasn't looking at the ornate nineteenth-century facade. He was looking at her.

"I wasn't talking about the house but about the way you just wrinkled up your nose."

"Just testing for a hint of spring," she explained shyly. "It wasn't there this morning. But come, sir," she added with a formality inspired by her surroundings, "you mean to turn a girl's head."

Instantly matching her mood, Roger twirled an imaginary moustache and replied, "And I intend to turn it even further by plying the pretty thing with drink."

They were smiling at each other in acknowledgment of the charade they had just enacted when Roger's expression changed abruptly. "Do you mind if I do something impetuous?" he asked.

Mollie looked puzzled, but without giving her a chance to answer he took the one step that separated them and softly brushed her lips with his. It was a skilled kiss, one that bespoke much experience, and it was not

at all unpleasant. But Mollie, who had earlier trembled
at the touch of his hands on her shoulder, was astonished
to find herself unmoved. Did she feel uncomfortable
about being kissed in the street? Angry at the casualness
of his approach? No. Instinctively she knew it was neither
of those reasons. She was hurt by the unmistakable lack
of warmth, by her sure sense that he intended the embrace
to create distance instead of closeness.

Just as she was about to break away, Roger let her
go. Before he could say anything, she asked coldly,
"What was that supposed to be?"

"I was wondering what your lips would feel like," he
answered lightly after a barely perceptible pause.

Mollie settled the strap of her handbag more securely
on her shoulder and put her hands in her pockets. They
were trembling slightly—in anger, not passion—but she
didn't want him to misunderstand. Making no effort to
hide her irritation, she retorted, "I'm not sure I like being
treated as if I were an experiment." Then curiosity got
the better of her anger. "And what have you decided?"
she found herself asking.

"I'm not sure yet," he replied slowly. "Let me try
again." Once more he did not wait for permission.

Mollie's first response was to resist, to pull away. But
he didn't let her. She was caught within the tight circle
of his arms, and after a moment she no longer wanted
to be free. Lightly, lightly—just as lightly as before—
his lips brushed hers, tracing the contours of her mouth,
then became more urgent, more demanding, sending a
message that flowed between them, a message so personal that Mollie felt in her every atom that it could only
be from him, Roger, to her, Mollie. As her eyes closed,
she became oblivious of the place, the people, the slight
chill in the air. But perhaps that was because her body
was now molded tightly against his. She could sense its
warmth penetrating her clothing to touch her everywhere.

"Something between fire and ice," he said, releasing

her at last, a slight puzzlement in his tone. "But I don't want to decide too hastily. The question will require further investigation." Now his voice was perfectly steady. Only his eyes betrayed his physical arousal—and even that he seemed to bring under control as she watched.

Mollie's mind was awhirl. She hadn't expected his kisses, and she was shaken by the strength of her physical response to him. It seemed incredible that she should react that way to a man about whom she knew so little. But what her eyes had seen from the first moment, her body had verified beyond doubt. Though they had spent less than half an hour together, she somehow felt that a lot had happened in that time. Just what, she couldn't precisely say—anymore than she could decide what that second kiss had meant to him.

He murmured into her ear. "Where *are* you taking me, Mollie?" His voice was husky, his breath warm. "Where *are* you taking me?"

Forcing herself to think clearly again, Mollie decided to answer his question literally, but she knew her response was ambiguous. "Wait and see."

This was evidently not what Roger had hoped to hear, but he managed to conceal—almost—a gesture of irritation as they continued along the park and headed down Irving Place to Pete's Tavern, a favorite neighborhood watering hole in the evening and a mecca for the area's literati at lunchtime.

Because they were so early, they had no trouble getting a table. As they settled into one of the booths in the paneled back room, Roger nodded approvingly as he took in their unpretentious surroundings. "Very clever," he commented.

Obviously he was going to ignore what had happened back there at the park. So be it. Mollie vowed not to be the first to bring it up.

"Clever?" she repeated. "What do you mean?"

"I mean it was perceptive of you to realize I wouldn't be impressed by a chic restaurant."

"I wasn't trying to impress you at all," Mollie objected. "Actually I was tempted to take you to the place across the street—it's both chic *and* good—but I thought you'd rather see O. Henry's old haunt."

"You say you were tempted, but you didn't follow through," Roger said, picking up on only the first part of her sentence. "Do you always put your escort's preferences first?"

Was he referring indirectly to their previous discussion about women being either jellyfish or piranha and asking if she was a jellyfish? Feeling that she was on dangerous ground, Mollie kept her answer impersonal. "That's what women have been taught to do," she remarked in a neutral tone.

His sharp angular face, alive with an almost ferocious intelligence, took fire. He leaned forward, eager to argue the point, but was interrupted when a waiter appeared for their drink orders. Roger asked for a scotch and water, but Mollie, feeling she had been on a roller coaster that morning, wanted only a Perrier with a twist of lime.

"I'll never be able to turn your head with such an innocent brew. Or with anything else, I gather," he added grimly, in what was perhaps an oblique reference to her response to his first kiss.

Could he be unaware of the effect of that second embrace? Did he think she was still angry about being an "experiment"? But before Mollie could pick up on this, he had moved on to another topic. "I thought all New York editors had nothing but martinis for lunch."

"Error number one. In any case, those who do are generally what's known in the trade as procuring editors."

He seized on the phrase with delight. "Procurors, are they? Shakespeare's term for pimp. It sounds fitting, but oddly enough I've never heard the term before—as applied to publishing, I mean."

"Well," she confessed, "the more usual term is 'acquiring editor,' but I often think the other is more accurate."

"And you? Are you an acquiring editor?"

"Sometimes. I'm more the ordinary garden or working variety."

"You never socialize with your authors?"

"Occasionally, but most often I do it only under pressure from Jim Lorne."

"Like now?" he demanded. "I suppose the fact that I did the inviting doesn't change the essential situation, does it?"

"Cards on the table?" she asked, looking him directly in the eye.

He nodded. "That's the way *I* like to play."

Mollie decided to let the barely disguised implication that she either couldn't or wouldn't be honest pass unchallenged. "I'm sure Jim isn't at all unhappy that we're lunching together. But as you noticed, *I* was willing enough—even though when I stormed out of his office earlier this morning I had pretty well decided that all commerce between us was over."

"What made you change your mind?" Roger's face was serious now. The hypnotizing voice had not a hint of laughter in it. His eyes—those eyes so alive to everything—sought hers questioningly, almost hostilely.

Mollie met his gaze for a moment, then looked down as the waiter returned with their drinks. Lifting the bit of peel from her glass, she took a tentative bite and was rewarded with the fresh taste and scent of lime.

"I'm not sure why I changed my mind," she said finally, "but I doubt if it had much to do with commerce. Let's just say I was exercising a woman's prerogative."

The laugh with which he greeted this comment was

harsh and unpleasant. His hand gripped his glass as he said angrily, "Leave it to women to find a fancy term to describe their lack of will. How would you describe a man who behaved similarly? Shall we try weak? Unprincipled?"

His expression and manner had become cold and arrogant, and Mollie was reminded that the man who sat opposite her was the same man who had expressed—with a verbal skill that was dangerously convincing—an extremely low opinion of her sex in a recent bestselling novel. She wondered what kinds of experiences with women had formed his view. Roger Herrick was an essentially honest man, she was convinced, who would not have written a lie unless he had first brought himself to believe it.

"Be that as it may," she said slowly, "it's unkind of you to reproach me for being here at your invitation." She was genuinely hurt. "And unfair," she added with a surge of anger.

"A lot of things in life are unfair, and you're likely to be sorry if you forget it."

"In that case, I guess it comes down to how you feel about that kind of injustice, doesn't it?" Giving him no time to answer, she added, "I think we'd better order. Even Jim Lorne might disapprove of this tête-à-tête if I'm out too long."

They selected their dishes from a blackboard menu hanging at the far end of the room—scampi for her and cannelloni for him. With their order the waiter brought a basket of garlic bread wrapped in a white-and-red-checked napkin and a schooner of light beer for Herrick.

Mollie was unhappy. Your wish is my command, he had said back at the office. True, the phrasing had been ironic, but she had felt his unmistakable interest. Even before those unexpected kisses he had been attentive, responsive . . . just like any man attracted to a woman. Mollie hadn't reached her present age without having her share of masculine attention, some of which she had certainly enjoyed. But she had never been wooed, or more likely mocked, so fiercely within an hour of meeting. Then, as soon as she had challenged him, he had become caustic, almost insolent. If this was his response to criticism, editing his book would be no easy task. And as for any relationship between them...

Roger too seemed absorbed in his own thoughts, and once their food arrived they ate for a while in silence. But it was an armed silence that indicated they were very aware of each other's presence.

"A penny," Mollie finally said when the waiter had brought their coffee.

Roger looked at her gravely, as though considering the offer. "For my thoughts? Are you sure you want to risk it?"

"I can afford it—even on what I get from Jim Lorne. But why so reluctant? Is what you're thinking so unflattering to me? Just because I disagreed with you?"

He laughed harshly. "That is definitely *not* what was on my mind! Do you really want to know? You're not just being coy?"

"Of course I do," she said seriously. "I'm twenty-nine years old and I'm *not* coy. Ever. I want to know. Do you really think me so awful?"

"Awful?" he repeated, shaking his head and smiling sardonically. "Now you're begging, Mollie. You know damn well that I don't find you any more awful than you find me."

Mollie gasped at his audacity—and was aghast at how transparent she must have been. She had thought he would refrain from mentioning their second kiss, but Roger obviously played by whatever rules he chose, skipping from the intellectual to the personal with the greatest of ease. "You're wrong, Roger," she said defiantly. "I don't know any such thing. All I know is that you're not quite what your books led me to expect."

"'Man's art is of man's life a thing apart,' as I'm sure you've heard."

"The line as written by Byron is 'Man's *love* is of man's life a thing apart.'"

"'Tis a woman's whole existence,'" he said, completing the quote. "You've caught me out." To Mollie's surprise, he seemed delighted. "But I wouldn't have thought," he continued, "that the idea of love being a woman's whole existence was a very popular one these days."

"Perhaps that's because women have found that staking everything on love is dangerous," she answered quickly. "And while a life without love is a dismal prospect, a woman who has no existence apart from the man she loves eventually becomes a burden to him."

As if standing on an imaginary soapbox, she plunged on. Tim had given her reason to feel strongly about the subject.... "Really, instead of complaining about unfeminine women," she said, "men ought to be grateful that more and more women are developing independent lives. It makes them much more interesting to be with."

"Just as I said," Roger snapped. "Having seen that subservience has failed, they're giving dominance a try."

Despite a sense of growing danger, Mollie rushed on impetuously. "As *you* see it! But you stack the cards. For example, take Jenny in your new novel. It's easy to understand why Jason tires of her. It's not enough for a woman to be beautiful and available."

"I'm afraid the book has bored you." His voice held more than a hint of anger.

"No, that's not true," she answered, realizing more fully how important his writing was to him, but determined to speak honestly. "It's not the portrait of Jenny I'm objecting to. She does exist—in your book and in the world. I've known women like her. The trouble is that she exists only when she's with Jason."

"Exactly." He leaned forward, his expression intent.

"When such a woman is in love, she draws her strength from the man. Eventually he find himself weakened and humiliated by the desire she creates in him."

"But love isn't like that," she insisted. "Not real love. And real women aren't like your Jenny."

"There's that charming feminine inconsistency again," he replied in a tone that clearly indicated he found it anything but charming. His eyes blazed, and his voice, though low, penetrated to the quick. "You just admitted that she exists! But I suspect"—he glared at her—"that inconsistency is part of women's basic nature. For example, they think they want lovers who are considerate and tender, but they reward only those who are impatient and aggressive."

"Paradox isn't an argument. Neither is irony," she replied quickly.

"Perhaps irony is one of the few weapons men have when faced with feminine inconsistency."

"You mean, I suppose, what I said about your Jenny. Actually, there was nothing inconsistent about my point of view." Mollie watched the play of emotions on his face, studying the strongly defined planes and angles— the pronounced cheekbones, the determined jawline, the well-defined lips—and found her fingers aching to trace them. His closeness was beginning to trouble her, but she was able to say firmly, "Jenny exists. I admitted I've known women like her, and I said you drew their portrait accurately."

"So?"

"My objection isn't to the portrait of Jenny but to the fact that you seem to be presenting her as a kind of Everywoman."

"Do you prefer my Amanda?"

"No. Amanda is another horror. She's determined to dominate, afraid to give."

"Not much to choose from, is there?" he pointed out, his face a hostile mask.

Mollie gathered herself for a final effort. "Don't you see that the choice isn't limited to the Jennies and the Amandas in the world?"

"I suppose you're thinking of yourself? Every woman assumes she's an exception." He examined her body—or as much as he could see of her across the table—closely, taking his time. "Not bad," he concluded dispassionately. "A fine mind, certainly, and quite attractively housed."

Under other circumstances Mollie might have been flattered or even flustered by this statement, but she could not forget that second kiss—which must have been a deliberate effort to prove her susceptibility—and she felt that his comment was meant to wound, not to compliment. Her strength rushed from her and she suddenly felt cold. It was no use. He could not—would not—understand.

Exasperated almost to the point of tears, Mollie clenched her fists so rigidly that the nails bent against her palms. She would *not* cry. He would see tears—any hint of tears—as a female ploy. When all else fails, women weep.

"Women," she began again, stubbornly determined to keep the argument on an intellectual level, "are not necessarily more inconsistent than men. We're all inconsistent at times, and if women seem more so it's because inconsistency is one of the few weapons men allow them."

"Enter the villain, man," he returned dryly. "And on the basis of what vast experience have you decided that men are at fault?"

"First of all I never said men were at fault. You put those words into my mouth. As for experience I, at least, have had several years of living with a member of the opposite sex on a day to day basis. Can you say as much, Roger?"

He glowered, and Mollie, immediately understanding

the significance of his look, hastened to add, "Oh, I'm not asking you to compare involvements. I just meant that I was once married. Sorry, I assumed you knew. Didn't Jim fill you in?"

"No, why should he have?"

"Because he's a blabbermouth and because he doesn't seem to appreciate my desire to keep my personal and my professional lives separate. At first it bothered me, but I've gotten used to it."

But Roger wasn't interested in discussing Jim Lorne. "What happened? With your marriage, I mean? Unless you'd rather not talk about it," he added.

"No, I don't mind." Only as she said the words did she realize they were true. She did *not* mind talking to Roger about her personal life. "Tim and I were divorced four years ago. These days it seems as if it happened a long time ago, and to somebody else."

He waited for her to continue. She could see that his interest was genuine, so she went on. "I suppose we were both too young. *I* certainly was. Twenty-three, one year out of college, sexually and emotionally inexperienced, terribly excited about being in New York and about the entry-level job I had just found in a publishing house." She paused. It was going to be more difficult than she had thought.

"I don't hear anything wrong so far," Roger said slowly. "As a matter of fact it sounds like a promising beginning."

Mollie looked up quickly to see if he was mocking her, but his gaze was serious and sympathetic. "Unfortunately, it didn't live up to its promise," she said, regretfully.

"What happened?" he urged.

"Do I have your word that this whole story won't show up in your next novel?" she asked with a nervous laugh.

"Surely you know what a novelist's word is worth in

such matters," he said with surprising gravity. "Everything is grist for the mill."

"Nevertheless, I know that if *you* gave me your word, you would keep it," she said without hesitation.

For a moment he made no reply. Then he said almost reluctantly, "Don't give me credit for being better than I am. But we were talking about you."

Mollie toyed with her empty coffee cup. "So we were," she said. "Actually, there's not all that much to say. I think Tim really loved me, at least at the beginning, but he could never get used to the fact that my work was as important to me as his was to him."

"Are you that committed to being a career woman?" Roger interrupted. "What about children?"

"We both wanted a family, but Tim wasn't ready to have children," Mollie replied, "and he was quite right. We were too young and the marriage too untested. The trouble was that in the meantime, he didn't really want a wife, a companion, a partner. He wanted someone who would always be available to do what he wanted when he wanted. He didn't object to my working. By the time we got married it was all right to have a working wife. But he didn't want me to take my work seriously. For instance he was a lawyer and would bring home briefs almost every evening. But on the few occasions when I had to bring a manuscript home he blew his top."

As she told the story Mollie felt her old anger reviving.

"Did he object to having an intelligent wife?" asked Roger with an intensity that puzzled her.

"No," Mollie answered bitterly. "Tim never objected to intelligence in women—only to their using it."

Roger laughed. "Now that's a line I cannot promise not to borrow for a novel someday."

"As long as I get mentioned in the acknowledgments," Mollie agreed.

Again they shared a moment of complete rapport, then

Roger said, "You were telling me what happened."

Mollie sighed. "Tim made it plain that we either played the game his way or didn't play at all. It was emotional blackmail, and by that time I wasn't buying. I'd already begun to see that the marriage wasn't going to work, that he wanted me to give up too much—not just my work, but almost everything that made me *me*—and I began to fight back."

"How?"

"Well, I not only rejected what I saw as his unreasonable requests, but I'm afraid I began to reject a lot of other things as well."

This was still a painful topic for Mollie, and she avoided Roger's eyes now—though she felt them on her, just as she could sense when something broke the connection between them.

She wasn't at all surprised to hear him say fiercely, "And so to avoid being a jellyfish you became a piranha."

Without giving her a chance to reply, he summoned the waiter impatiently. While he was occupied in paying the check, Mollie had time to get a grip on herself and recover from the shock of his last words, which had been like a slap in the face. It was as though she had been abruptly ejected from the comfort of his presence to the desolation of his absence. . . . When he helped her into her coat she was aware that this time he avoided touching her, and they were both silent during their walk back to the office.

As they reached the brownstone that housed Lorne Publications, Mollie drew herself up to her full height and looked Roger directly in the eye. "And you, Roger," she said deliberately. "What about you? Does an intelligent woman using her intelligence seem such an unbearable challenge to you too?"

Now she had done it. The silence that followed seemed interminable.

"Perhaps you're not the right one after all," he said finally, his voice level but drained of all emotion.

"The right one?" she asked confused.

"To edit my book, of course," he snapped. "As a matter of fact, given your many objections, maybe you ought to write a book of your own."

"I just might," she replied tartly. But the fight had gone out of her. All she wanted was to get away without letting him hurt her again.

"And now I'd better give you back to Jim Lorne," he said. "Thanks for joining me for lunch. And for showing me"—he hesitated—"Pete's Tavern."

Numbly she put out her hand in response to his gesture of farewell—of dismissal. Earlier that day, a lifetime earlier, her hand had nestled briefly in his warm one and she had withdrawn it regretfully. Now she was relieved when he released her and turned away.

"Anything wrong, honey?" Betty asked solicitously as Mollie passed her desk.

"Nothing much," she threw back over her shoulder. "It's just that I feel like I've been hit by a Mack truck."

Betty started up in alarm.

"Relax, Betty, relax. It's only a joke. I've just had a working lunch with Roger Herrick."

"But that should have been fun," Betty protested.

"It should have been," Mollie agreed.

"He looks like a difficult type," Betty ventured. "The thing is you've got to know how to treat a man."

Mollie whirled to face her angrily. "Isn't it time men started learning how to treat women?" But Betty looked so hurt by her outburst that Mollie immediately apologized.

"Sure, honey, sure. I understand," the older woman said reassuringly. "I still remember how they can twist you around until . . ." Her voice faded into silence.

Back in her office Mollie surveyed the pile of work she had meant to get through that day, including Larry Lambert's introduction to his new volume of verse. Picking up her blue pencil, she suppressed a shudder and went to work. She would have to remember to explain— if she could find a way that didn't offend his sensitive male ego—the correct grammatical use of *lay* and *lie*. She sighed. You'd think the oversexed boy genius would know that *lay* always requires an object.

After a few minutes she shoved the manuscript away from her in disgust and walked over to the window. A gray drizzle was falling, and she felt as if she were inside an aquarium. The weather was as dismal as it had been that morning. Where was the hint of spring she thought she had spotted earlier?

As she turned back to her desk, her eye caught the mauve envelope from Odette. Picking it up, she fanned herself with it until the scent of heliotrope became too much for her.

April in Paris! Why not? All of a sudden she felt an overwhelming urge to get away. She had a lot of vacation time coming to her, and she'd add some unpaid leave. Jim would object, of course, but if he didn't like it, he could lump it. She'd do it!

Lifting the phone before she could change her mind, Mollie dialed the cable office, humming to herself while she waited. Yes, what she needed right now was a change of scene. She was tired of feeling like an editor. Paris would make her feel like a woman again.

"I'd like to send a cable to Paris," she said when the clerk answered. "It goes to Madame Odette Gerard, nineteen rue Monge. The message is as follows: 'Enroll me in first session of Gerard Ecole de Cuisine.'" She stopped, fumbling on her desk for a calendar. It was Friday the thirteenth, of course! "'Arriving Paris April twenty,'" she went on. "'Can you get me someplace to stay for six weeks? *A bientôt.'* I'll spell that for you, operator." She did. "That's signed, 'Love Mollie.' "

Love Mollie, she thought as she hung up. Will the real man who can love the real Mollie Paine please stand up. She's been waiting a long time.

- *3* -

"MADEMOISELLE PAINE! Mademoiselle Paine! You're wanted on the telephone."

Still struggling to wake up, Mollie called through the door, *"Très bien,* Monsieur Robinet, I'll be right down."

What time was it, she wondered, groping under the pillow for her watch. Only 7:30. Who would be calling her at that hour? As a matter of fact who would be calling her, period?

When she'd first moved into this tiny studio, she'd been worried about the lack of a phone—a lack that was by no means rare in Paris, as she'd soon learned. But the concierge had said he'd be glad to call her to his phone whenever necessary, and so far, after almost a week, her only calls had been from Odette Gerard, who made it a point of honor never to get up before noon. "Everything bad that's ever happened to me," Odette had explained, "has always happened before *midi,* so I only increase the risks if I get up earlier."

Hastily pulling on her robe and shoving her feet into a pair of slippers, Mollie stumbled to the door and down to the concierge's *loge.*

"From America," he said, greeting her excitedly at his door.

Mollie reached for the phone with a stab of guilt. There had been so many details to attend to before leaving for France that she hadn't had time to go down to Philadelphia and say goodbye to her folks. When she'd

41

phoned to say she was leaving in a few days, her mother had been so anxious about her father, sick with the flu, that she hadn't even had the energy to scold Mollie. Could her father be worse?

"Hello?" she said tremulously into the mouthpiece of the old-fashioned phone, adjusting the receiver to her ear.

"Mollie?"

"Jim Lorne!" she exploded in exasperated relief. "Do you know what time it is here?"

"Well, I wanted to make sure I'd catch you before you started on your merry rounds. How's Paris?"

"You didn't wake me at seven-thirty in the morning just to ask me that, did you?"

"No, but I thought it might do for openers. In any case Betty said that if I spoke to you I was to be sure to ask, so I'm asking."

"Well, tell her Paris isn't the Big Apple, but at least it doesn't have the worm."

"You mean me, I suppose?"

"If the shoe fits . . ."

"You've entirely misread my character."

"I didn't know you had any."

"That is no way to speak to the only publisher in New York who would allow his number one editor to leave her desk for six weeks. And by the way, how *is* that madwoman's cooking school?"

"There isn't any."

Monsieur Robinet leaned closer, not even trying to hide his interest in the conversation, though Mollie knew his English wasn't up to it. As she settled down for what was obviously going to be an extended transatlantic call, she could practically *hear* him trying to calculate how much it would cost. Crazy Americans! And rich, she knew he must be thinking.

"I said there isn't any cooking school. It was a *poisson d'avril.*"

"What kind of poison?"

"You heard me, Jim. Not poison, *poisson*—a fish. *Poisson d'avril*—April Fool, to you."

Mollie described how she had been met at the airport by a tearful Odette suffering from belated guilt. It had been the beginning of April, she had explained, Paris was lovely, and she was feeling old and alone. After consoling herself with a bottle of Moët champagne that she had been saving for a special occasion, she remembered it was April Fool's Day, had a sudden inspiration, and sent Mollie that letter.

"You understand, *ma chérie*," Odette had continued, "it was all so real to me that for a moment it was as though my lifelong dream had come true. But you really are the first pupil I would have chosen." Mollie, longing for escape, had accepted what some part of her must have known all along was an impossible story.

". . . eight, nine, ten," Jim was counting softly. Then he erupted: "And for this you ran off, leaving me up to my sideburns in unedited manuscripts?"

"I left you with nothing," Mollie spluttered. "I finished everything I had to do on the Lambert book. I cleaned up all the material that had to go to or was back from the printer. And you took the Herrick book away from me, remember?"

"Ah yes. The Herrick book. That brings me to the reason for this call. He's changed his mind, Mollie. Now he says that if you *don't* do the editing, he's going to take the book to Random House."

Jim paused for a moment, then continued in the off-hand manner Mollie recognized as his way of announcing big news. "As a matter of fact, he flew off to Paris with the manuscript a few hours ago. He should be landing there just about now. So, Mollie, what I want you to do . . ."

Mollie had stopped listening. Roger Herrick in Paris!

". . . he'll probably be knocking at your door this very

morning. He has your address and he said he'd take a taxi straight to your place from the airport."

"But he can't do that!" she all but screamed into the mouthpiece. Monsieur Robinet looked alarmed.

"Why not?"

Because I look and feel like a Raggedy Ann doll, she almost blurted out. Catching herself in time, she said instead, "Because I'm on vacation. The first one I've had in three years."

"Look," said Jim, ignoring her protest, "no arguments, please. It's the middle of the night here—or early in the morning to be precise—and I've got to catch some sleep before showing up at the office. Somebody's got to take care of the store. Anyway, this call is becoming too expensive even for me."

"But Jim—"

"Don't forget I expect you back in this office at nine o'clock sharp on June first," he interrupted. "And you'd better have Herrick in tow. Goodbye, love." He hung up.

"Anything wrong?" Monsieur Robinet asked anxiously as Mollie rushed past him and up the stairs.

"Everything's fine," she replied grimly. "Just peachy."

Back in the studio she sank down onto the unmade bed and surveyed the room with a feeling of desperation. It was almost eight o'clock now, and assuming Roger Herrick's flight was the same one she had taken a week earlier, and further assuming he did as Jim had said and came directly from the airport, he couldn't be here much before nine-thirty or ten.

There was, of course, also the off chance that Jim, after hearing about Odette's April Fool joke, had been inspired to pull a belated one of his own. But she couldn't take a chance. Besides, she acknowledged, Jim didn't joke about work.

What should she do first? Shower, she decided, and headed for the tiny bathroom that adjoined her only slightly less tiny studio. While she waited for the water to run hot, she told herself that Roger Herrick had no right to intrude on her vacation, that he was overbearing and too used to getting his way, that he...but in all honesty she had to admit that her heart wasn't beating wildly out of anger.

Soaping vigorously under the shower, she asked herself what exactly she did feel about Roger Herrick. When she tried to think about him, all she could conclude was that there seemed to be several Roger Herricks and that she'd met them all on that one morning.

He was a man of intelligence and wit who was secure enough to enjoy their spirited exchanges—at least until they struck too close to home. He was a man whose experience with women was obviously extensive, and who nevertheless was determined to misunderstand the very nature of love. And last but not least, she admitted, he was a man whose touch on her shoulder she could still feel, whose street-corner embrace had aroused more passion in her than she had ever known, whose eyes probed to her depths and left her trembling...

The trembling, she realized with a start, could also be attributed to the fact that she was still standing in a none-too-warm bathroom wrapped only in a green bath towel—an outfit in which she could hardly receive whichever of the Roger Herricks would finally show up at her door.

And yet, she thought, emerging into the main room and surveying herself in the full-length mirror that fronted the door of the armoire in which her clothes were hung, the effect was not at all unappealing....Too bad she wasn't prepared to play that game.

With a sigh she swung open the armoire and began to rifle frantically among the hangers. My God! She must have been mad to come to Paris with two suitcases crammed full of clothes she didn't want to wear!

Rushing to the window, she flung open the two panels

and leaned out. Below was a charming inner courtyard, immaculately clean and dotted here and there with potted plants. Above was a patch of misty sky in which the sun was struggling to dissipate the slight morning fog.

It still felt marvelous to be here, and she didn't regret a thing, she thought happily. Only the sound of a neighbor's radio announcing the time roused her to action. It was eight twenty-seven, and she was still wearing only a green towel.

Stopping on her way back to the armoire, she paused long enough to make the bed and pick up the clothes she'd worn the night before. By the time she'd finished, she'd decided what to wear, and she dressed quickly in a black knit jersey skirt and a pale green crepe de chine blouse. If she wore her dark-green sweater coat, she'd be ready for whatever the changeable April weather would bring.

And that would have to do, she concluded. It was adolescent to get so excited about dressing for Roger Herrick. Nostalgically, she thought of her college days, when her wardrobe consisted of blue jeans, shirts and sweaters. A lot could be said for that kind of life. Women would probably never be truly liberated until they freed themselves from the morning hassle of deciding what to wear. It was undignified—and besides, it was unlikely that Roger would ever notice. No, that wasn't so. She retracted the thought. Something told her that *nothing* escaped Roger Herrick's critical eyes.

Mollie had just added a long string of amber beads and slipped into her black pumps when a sharp rap sounded on the door. Catching her breath, she stood perfectly still for a moment and considered whether or not she would answer. No, she wouldn't answer. Given the way they had parted, meeting Roger Herrick again could bring her nothing but grief.

The knock came again, more peremptorily. "Mollie!"

It was his voice. She had heard it on only one other

day in her life but she would remember it always. Struggling to get a grip on herself, she slowly walked toward the door and flung it open.

The ceiling fixture in the windowless hallway was controlled by a *minuterie,* a penny-saving switch which, when pressed, turned on the electricity for just a minute before everything was plunged again into darkness. And so it happened that when she opened the door she got only a quick glimpse of Roger before the light went out and he became only a dim outline. First you see him, then you don't, Mollie thought. How apropos. She fumbled behind her for the light switch in her room and suddenly he was there again.

"Aren't you going to invite me in?" he asked as she continued to stare at him in silence. "I've come a long way to do penance."

"Is that what you've come for?" she asked suspiciously, stepping aside to allow him in.

"Of course," he replied lazily. "I decided that though your views on women in love conflict with mine—and are completely wrong—"

"That doesn't sound like the beginning of a penitential speech," she interrupted.

"You could hardly expect me to come barefoot and dressed in sackcloth and ashes, could you?"

"To tell the truth I didn't expect you at all—at least not until about an hour ago."

"Lorne got in touch with you, did he? He promised me he wouldn't."

"If you remember, I've already told you not to put too much stock in Jim Lorne's promises."

"I remember—everything."

He looked at her the way he had just before he had kissed her that second time, and the memory gave her the courage to fight the impulse to lower her eyes. With an effort that was slowly transmuted into pleasure, she steadily returned his gaze. Damn, but the man was attractive! He stood in the middle of a strange room, with a woman he had been with for less than three hours, and already he seemed completely at home, completely in charge—and completely electrifying.

"You know," he said casually, as though returning to a previous conversation, "sometimes you do or say something that really intrigues me." She caught her breath, but he continued without giving her a chance to speak. "For example, both my Jenny and my Amanda would have, for different reasons, pretended to be flustered by my 'unexpected' arrival."

"You should have seen me an hour or so ago, when I first got the news that you were on your way," she replied, finding once again that she wanted to be completely honest with him, no matter what it cost her. "But now that you're here, suppose you tell me why you've really come."

"I told you—penance. And perhaps because we speak the same language, even though so far we tend to do little else but argue in it."

"Very clever," she snapped, determined not to let him see how closely what he had just said echoed her own feelings. "Are you going to use that line in your next book?"

Paying no attention to either her question or the note of belligerence in her voice, he lowered himself onto the dangerously torn seat of a canvas director's chair and surveyed the studio. Mollie mentally made the inventory with him—a brown foam rubber studio couch, a small white chest of drawers, an armoire that served as the room's only closet, some bookshelves, and a waist-high refrigerator and two-burner stove tucked into a corner alcove. On one wall was a large turn-of-the-century photograph of the corner at which the boulevard Saint-Michel met the Seine, Notre Dame looming in the background.

"Nice," he concluded. "But I wouldn't have thought that a woman could be happy in such a—a *basic* place."

"Places are less important to women than the people they share them with," Mollie retorted.

One dark eyebrow raised, he looked at her intently, as if to ask, And with whom are you sharing this place? Then, seemingly satisfied with what he saw, he merely said, "How did you find it?"

"Odette Gerard found it for me. It belongs to a friend who's moved to something better but isn't quite ready to give this up and was happy to rent it."

"Gerard? Oh yes, your gourmet cook. Lorne told me about her. How's that working out?"

Mollie broke into a frank laugh. "I'm afraid the joke's on me." And she told him about the April Fool ploy, adding wryly, "It turns out that while Odette does know a great deal about food, she's much more interested in consuming it than preparing it. Left to herself, she doesn't cook; she just heats."

Roger Herrick's rich laughter filled the tiny room, and the atmosphere became suddenly relaxed, even intimate—perhaps too much so, because Mollie found herself saying nervously, "Would it be too forward of me to suggest that you buy me some breakfast? I'm starving."

He rose to his feet almost immediately, but Mollie sensed his reluctance to leave. "Come to think of it, so am I. But I'm also dog tired." He glanced swiftly at the couch, then back at her, but evidently decided against pursuing whatever ideas he had had.

If he was tired, he certainly didn't look it. Considering that he'd spent the night on a plane, it was amazing that his brown corduroy jacket and chino pants were completely unrumpled, his yellow shirt still fresh-looking, and he himself totally awake and alert. He wore his masculinity easily, conveying a strength that suggested he did not become tired from activities that exhausted most other people.

He reached for the musette bag he had dropped on the

floor. "Here," he said, opening it. "Read it when you get a chance."

"Your manuscript?"

He nodded. "I'd like you to finish it," he said without further explanation.

"Of course," Mollie replied. But she was puzzled by his tone. "Where did you leave your things?"

He patted the bag.

"Is that all your luggage?" she asked in disbelief.

"I'm afraid so. And as you can see, most of it was the manuscript. I came directly from New York, without going back to Chicago. I'll pick up whatever I need here."

"Where are you staying?"

Silently he once more surveyed the studio, his eyes finally coming to rest on Mollie. "This place was rented to me as 'suitable for one,'" she said quickly.

"I can imagine it doing very well for a 'loving two.'"

Instead of answering, Mollie reached for her sweater coat and opened the door to the hallway. "There's a nice cafe at the Ecole Militaire, just a few blocks from here."

"Pitiless woman." He sighed with exaggerated emphasis and moved toward the door.

As Mollie and Roger left the building, they brushed past Mollie's next-door neighbor, Madame Renal, and her young son, Jean-Pierre. The lady glanced at them shyly, murmured a soft *bonjour,* and continued toward the stairway.

"You seem quite at home here," said Roger.

Mollie agreed. "I love this neighborhood so much that I can almost forgive Odette for bringing me to Paris on false pretenses."

As they walked she told him about rue de Grenelle, the narrow street on which she lived. Only a short walk from the Seine, and a shorter walk from the Eiffel Tower, it cut a swath through the Left Bank from the Champ-de-Mars in the elegant seventh arrondissement to the rue des Saints Pères in the lively sixth, changing its character as it meandered along. The section Mollie lived—in had a provincial charm. It was, in fact, almost a small town to itself.

The narrow streets nearby were filled with the shops of artisans and with small, inexpensive, and always crowded restaurants. Odette had dismissed them as *gargotes,* slop shops fit only for the working class. When Mollie had protested that she herself was a member of that despised majority, Odette had said, "Nonsense! Americans don't *work* for money, they *have* money."

Roger listened attentively as Mollie spoke, remaining silent until they were settled at a small table on the outdoor terrace and had ordered large *cafés crèmes* and a basket of croissants. Finally he asked, "Have you been happy here?"

It was a question she hadn't dared ask herself. "Frankly, I don't know," she hedged. "I love the city, of course, and at last I really have the time to get to know it. I expect to register for some language courses next week, which I'm looking forward to starting. Odette's been very kind . . ." Her voice trailed off.

"But?"

She hesitated. Then, seeing that he was looking at her with genuine interest, she decided to say it all. "You're going to think me silly and I probably am, but I can't help feeling that April in Paris would be even more wonderful if . . . if I shared it with someone."

"And you're quite alone?"

"Pretty much so, except for Odette. I've become friendly with Madame Renal, and I suppose I could always look up some of the people I met last year at the French publishing houses . . . but I really wanted to get away from business."

"Speaking of business," he interrupted brusquely, "I may as well confess that you weren't the only reason I came to Paris."

She looked at him inquiringly.

"I'm supposed to meet with Annie Dumont, the woman who did the French translation of *The Weaker Sex*. She did a good job, and I've asked that she do the new book too. I sent her a copy of my *Woman in Love* manuscript so she could get some idea of it in advance."

The name Annie Dumont sounded vaguely familiar to Mollie, but she couldn't place it exactly. She'd probably seen it in the office on some of the contracts for Lorne books that had been sold to French publishers.

"Annie wrote me a long and rather complicated letter about some possible translation problems," Roger went on. "She feels that if she's really going to do a top-notch job, we ought to discuss some specific points before she starts."

"She may be right," Mollie agreed in a guarded tone.

"Depends on what she has in mind," Roger said ambiguously. "In any event, I'm grateful to her for giving me an excuse to come."

"I thought penance was the reason," Mollie retorted swiftly, surprised to feel hurt by his revelation.

"The Internal Revenue Service isn't strong on penance as a reason for business travel," he replied laconically. Looking directly at Mollie, he continued, "If you're able to change my mind about anything, I can give Annie the new material while I'm here."

Mollie recognized the challenge in his voice. "I wonder if I dare have another of these croissants?" she said, to give herself a chance to think.

Roger laughed, and, to her dismay, Mollie blushed.

"All right," he gave in. "We won't say any more about it now. Shall we get down to planning my first day in Paris?"

Mollie wasn't sure whether or not to take his comment as an invitation to spend the day together. "I have a pretty good guide book I could lend you," she said noncommittally. When she looked across the tiny table at him—they were sitting so close they were almost touching—

she saw at once that he was frankly enjoying himself, possibly because of the pleasure he took in being in control of the situation.

"Why take a guide book when I can have a guide? I can, Mollie, can't I?"

"You mean me, I suppose," she retorted. "I must say you take a lot for granted. Suppose I have other plans, suppose—"

"Don't spoil it, Mollie. You were just honest enough to tell me you knew nobody in Paris." He leaned across the table and took her hand in his. "Let's not play games," he said insistently. "Just say yes." His lips quirked upward as he added, "If it makes you feel better, you can spend your time trying to convince me that I'm wrong about female psychology."

There it was again—the maddening combination of gravity and mockery. Well, she didn't care. He was right. Why play games? Spending this beautiful day with Roger Herrick struck her as exactly what she wanted to do.

"Agreed. Shall we begin with a stroll along the Seine to Notre Dame?" she asked, quick enthusiasm sweeping all doubts aside. "We can pick up some food on rue Saint-Dominique and maybe have a picnic lunch when we get to that little park at the tip of the Île de la Cité."

"Sounds like an innocent enough beginning," he said, tossing some coins down on the table and reaching for his musette bag. "And somewhere along the way I can find a hotel and drop this. Okay? Let's go."

"Not in *these* shoes," she objected. "That's serious walking I have in mind. We'll have to go back to the studio so I can change into a pair of flats."

When they arrived at her door, Mollie searched frantically in her bag for her key. "I hope I haven't lost it. Odette had only one, and the concierge doesn't have a duplicate." With a sigh of relief, she extricated a key from the mass of small objects at the bottom of her purse and hastily opened the door.

Two enormous Vuitton suitcases stood in the middle of the studio, and from the adjoining bathroom they heard the shower running. Mollie, puzzled, looked at Roger and found that his face had become a mask from which his eyes shone like blazing coals.

"Is that you, darling?" a male voice called from the next room. "I just got here. Let myself in with my key. Be out in a minute."

As she watched, Roger's eyes turned icy cold.

- 4 -

MOLLIE STOOD STOCK-STILL, as though, like Lot's wife, she had been turned into a pillar of salt. There was a man in her shower and she had no idea who he was, but strangely enough that wasn't what bothered her. He didn't sound dangerous, and in any case she wasn't alone.

Or was she? Roger was still standing next to her, but he had totally withdrawn from her, and once again she recognized that his spiritual absence could be felt as strongly as his presence. She *was* alone, after all. Obviously he believed she'd lied to him—that whoever was in the shower must have entered with a key she'd given him, and that he was therefore probably her lover.

"Roger," she began, "it's not what you think. I can't begin to explain this yet, but—"

"Don't worry, something will occur to you," he said with glacial precision. "You've been caught a bit off balance, but I'm sure you'll soon think of some plausible explanation. You professional women are especially good at that kind of thing."

The scorn in his voice made her cringe inside. Surely he would soon see that she was telling the truth.

"But I tell you I haven't the faintest idea what's going on, Roger, or who that man—"

Before she could finish the sentence the bathroom door opened and Larry Lambert emerged, freshly scrubbed and smiling, a towel wrapped around his boyish waist.

As startled as she was, Mollie couldn't help but be amused by the bold designer signature embroidered over the spot where Larry's bellybutton should be.

"Why, hello there, Mollie," he said, evidently as surprised to see her as she was to see him.

"Mollie, this is obviously Monsieur Yves Saint-Laurent come to complete his new spring collection," Roger said caustically.

Ignoring him, Mollie snapped, "Larry, what the hell are you doing here?"

The boy wonder was about to reply when Roger interrupted. "Given the situation, I'm glad to see that you two do know each other after all." His voice was deliberately insolent, almost insulting.

"Yes, of course, I know him," Mollie replied impatiently. "This is Larry Lambert. Larry, this is Roger Herrick. And now that the formalities are out of the way, would you mind telling me how you got in here?"

"With the key I was given," Larry answered sulkily, readjusting the towel with a nervous gesture. It was clear that Roger's presence made him uncomfortable. Without *all* of his designer clothes, Larry seemed to lack an important prop for his self-assurance.

"You see, Mollie," Roger volunteered in an exaggeratedly pleasant tone, "it's all perfectly simple. He merely made use of the key you gave him."

"But I never—"

"I'm afraid my being here makes the situation rather awkward, Mr. Lambert," Roger said, cutting Mollie short and turning to Larry. "Mollie obviously had no idea that you were going to pay her a visit this morning, but don't worry. No great harm's been done." He put out his hand. "It *is* Larry Lambert the poet, isn't it?"

"Why yes," Larry replied with a pleased smile, extending his right hand while keeping his left tightly clutching the towel.

"I thought you might be, and I was sure you would turn out to be one of Jim Lorne's authors." Turning to Mollie, Roger said, a cutting edge in his voice, "It seems you are a successful procuring editor after all."

His words flicked through the air, and Mollie's cheeks burned as though she had been slapped. "Roger—"

"I think the best way to end our mutual embarrassment," he interrupted, "is for me to pick this up"—he retrieved his manuscript from the shelf—"and leave as quickly as possible."

"Roger, please listen—"

"Thanks for joining me for breakfast, Mollie. Our meetings seem fated to be punctuated by delightful . . . meals."

"Won't you wait until I can explain?" she said, despising herself for the note of pleading that had entered her voice.

He quietly but efficiently steamrollered right over her. "There's no need to explain. If anything, I'm the one who should apologize. I made a mistake."

"Roger, I swear—"

"Don't. It's unbecoming in a woman and it might turn Mr. Lambert off."

He obviously didn't intend to let her get a word in edgewise, and his flippant tone, meant to wound, was even more hurtful than his earlier anger. Mollie fought an impulse to slap his face.

Turning to Larry, Roger said with an icy but polite formality, "Goodbye, Lambert. I'm sure we'll be seeing each other. We seem to be attracted to . . . the same circles."

The door had hardly closed when Mollie whirled on her still dripping visitor. "You'd better have a damn good explanation for this, Larry Lambert!"

"I don't know if I *can* explain," he replied, running his fingers through the damp curls of his carefully shaped coiffure. "That is, without impugning the honor of a lady." He accompanied this high-sounding sentence with the kind of disagreeable leer Mollie associated with some of the boys she'd known back in college—most of them jocks whose brains had been in their biceps and who'd ask if she "wanted to neck" and, without waiting for an answer, lunge at her in a way that revealed a decided ignorance of anatomy as well as a lack of skill.

"The fact is," said Larry, after opening his suitcases and selecting several articles of clothing, with which he retreated behind the bathroom door, "I had no idea you lived here—or even that you were in Paris. What *are* you doing here?"

"Vacationing," Mollie said shortly. "And having a wonderful time, though I wish you weren't here."

"'*Satirical maids, you've met your match,*'" intoned Larry from behind the door. "'*I tell you plain this puss can scratch.*'" He laughed. "Do you like that rhyme? I wrote it after our last meeting."

"It's great," Mollie replied impatiently, "but would you mind getting back to your explanation of how you happen to be in my studio?"

"As far as I know," Larry called out, "this place belongs to a lady with whom I'm on friendly terms when I'm in this town." He tossed out his towel and asked that she stick it into one of his Vuittons.

"You don't mean Odette Gerard?" Mollie asked in disbelief as she complied.

"No, that's not her name—though I *have* met that weirdo."

Larry emerged from the bathroom looking like a walking billboard: the pink golf shirt with an alligator was a Lacoste, the boots screamed Frye, and when he turned to take his Patek Philippe watch off the shelf, Mollie read Calvin Klein on his backside. When Larry died, he'd probably be buried in a Bill Blass shroud, Mollie concluded.

"Hell," said Larry, "there's no reason to make such a big deal about it, I guess." She sensed he was actually eager to tell her. "The lady's name is Annie Dumont. She's the one who translated my last book of poems— you know, *Haight-Ashbury Agonies*. We got to know each other pretty well"—he was smiling that unpleasant smile again—"and she gave me a key to the place." Larry dug into his tight jean pockets and held up a shining key. "She said I was welcome at any time, and since I was restless back home I decided to come over and play in Paris for a while."

"Well, Annie doesn't live here anymore," Mollie said, swiftly plucking the key from his hand. She frowned. Of course. Odette had said that the studio belonged to a woman called Annie Dumont. That was why the name had sounded familiar when Roger had mentioned it earlier that morning.

Annie Dumont was *his* translator too, Mollie remembered with a sinking heart—but since Roger had never seen this place before, she thought with reviving spirits, *they* obviously didn't have the same arrangement.

Her feeling of relief was short-lived, however. Hadn't Odette said that Annie Dumont had recently gone on to better things? Maybe that meant Annie and Roger usually met in plusher surroundings. And if they did? she asked herself. What business was it of hers? And hadn't Roger been quite open with her? Hadn't he said he had come to Paris primarily at Annie's request? Or had he said that that was just an excuse for coming to see *her*, Mollie?

Why was life so complicated? She had to get rid of Larry so she could think it all through.

"*Voilà*," said the boy bard, tearing himself away from his reflection in the armoire mirror and the agonized examination of an imagined pimple. "Now I'm ready to enjoy April in Paris with you. A walk along the Seine, maybe a picnic lunch somewhere..."

He said the words innocently, but if he'd intended to

hurt her he couldn't have succeeded better. That was exactly how she and Roger had planned to spend the morning.

". . . and before you know it, it will be evening and the real fun will begin." Larry, totally oblivious to the problem he had created or to how Mollie was feeling, looked at her expectantly, then held out his right arm. "Shall we dance?" he asked.

If only Roger had given Larry the chance to explain!

Mollie started to sink wearily onto the couch, thought better of a gesture that might seem too inviting, and seated herself gingerly in the torn canvas chair. "I'm sorry, Larry, but I'm in no mood for any of that. You'd better run off and find your real lady love."

"She can wait. 'When I'm not near the girl I love,'" he sang, "'I love the girl I'm near.'"

"So I've noticed."

"And besides, if Annie doesn't live here anymore, I have no idea where to find her."

Mollie was going to say something about Roger probably being able to help him, but she decided against it.

"Larry," she pleaded, "I really would appreciate it if you would go now."

Something in her voice must have caught his attention because he looked at her sharply. "This Herrick guy someone special to you?"

Someone special. Yes, Roger was "someone special" to her. Though she had met him only twice and both meetings had ended badly, she knew with a certainty she couldn't deny that Roger Herrick meant a great deal to her.

"I'd rather not discuss it."

"Okay," he said flippantly, "but you'll break out in pimples if you go on this way." As though reminded of something, he gave a final anxious glance in the mirror before moving toward the door.

"Mind if I leave my Vuittons here? I'll send for them

as soon as I know where I'm staying." He looked around the studio. "It's cute," he began, "but the Right Bank is really more my style. Don't you think so?" he concluded hopefully.

"Larry, please go away." Mollie sighed wearily.

He turned to inspect her. "You're not looking too spry, Mollie *mon amour*," he said, mouthing the French words with exaggerated care.

Mollie had reached the end of her patience. "Not surprising, since I'm feeling anything *but* spry," she snapped. "As a matter of fact," she added bitterly, "if I weren't so lethargic, I'd think about committing suicide."

"All right, all right—I can take a hint. But are you sure you want to be alone?"

Mollie was again busy with her own thoughts and merely nodded.

Larry's hand was already on the door when he exclaimed, "Roger Herrick! *The* Roger Herrick?"

At Mollie's acknowledgment he gave a long whistle of surprise, stepped back into the room, walked over to her, and bent down to give her a kind, brotherly kiss on the top of her head. "Don't worry, Mollie," he said in a sympathetic voice that for some reason shocked her. "He'll feel like a simp when he realizes the mistake he's made."

No doubt he would; but how would he ever find out? And even if he did, how would he feel about her then? Feeling "like a simp" was not an emotion Roger Herrick would be very familiar with, nor one he would find easy to deal with.

Totally exhausted, Mollie leaned incautiously back in the chair. A loud, prolonged ripping sound accompanied the movement as the weary canvas finally gave way, and she let out a short, sharp yelp of surprise as she tried to keep from being pitched onto the floor.

Almost immediately she heard hurried footsteps in the

hall corridor, followed by an anxious knocking on her door.

"Mademoiselle Paine! Mademoiselle Paine! Are you all right?" It was her next-door neighbor.

"I'm fine, Madame Renal," Mollie called before opening the door. "The canvas on my chair split, and I almost had a nasty fall." She smiled at the young woman. "It's nice of you to be concerned. Won't you come in for a moment?"

Madame Renal looked pleased at the invitation. "Well, just for a moment. Jean-Pierre's asleep and I don't like to leave him alone. He hasn't been well lately and I'm worried."

"I'm sorry to hear that," Mollie murmured sympathetically. "Is there anything I can do?"

"No, thank you," said the shy widow as she inspected the torn seat of the director's chair. "You know, I'm sure I can fix that for you. Let me just run back and get a special needle. I'll leave my door open so I can hear when Jean-Pierre wakes up."

In a few moments, Madame Renal returned with a thimble, a thick needle, and some heavy thread. Seating herself on the couch, she drew the chair toward her and began to stitch expertly. "What a handsome man that was with you this morning," she noted conversationally.

"Do you think so?"

"Oh yes. In some ways he reminded me of François, my late husband." Madame Renal's thimbled right hand paused for a moment as she looked up from her sewing into a far distance. "Not that they really look alike," she went on, resuming her work. "It's just that they both seemed so strong, so capable. Ah, Mademoiselle Paine, if you had only known him. He stood so firm upon the earth." Her eyes glowed at the recollection.

"How did he die?" Mollie asked gently.

Madame Renal sighed. "There was a fire at the plant

he worked in. François was helping to evacuate some of
the men overcome by smoke, and suddenly a portion of
the roof caved in." She began weeping silently, without
embarrassment.

"How terrible!" Mollie breathed.

"Yes," she agreed, making an effort to compose herself. "He never even saw his son. Jean-Pierre was born
a month later."

Mollie felt ashamed of herself. She had been thinking,
how terrible for Madame Renal, alone with an infant.
But the young widow had been thinking only of her dead
husband.

"Oh, if you could have seen him," Madame Renal
continued, her face animated. "Always lively. We used
to go dancing every Saturday night, and when he held
me in his arms I felt so safe, so sure that nothing could
harm me."

The two women fell silent for a moment, each lost
in her own thoughts.

"But you're in love with him!" the widow unexpectedly
said softly, looking at Mollie attentively. "I hope I'm not
being indiscreet, mademoiselle," she added swiftly.

"Oh, please, won't you call me Mollie? Mademoiselle
sounds so formal."

"With pleasure," her neighbor replied. "And I am
Madeleine."

They smiled at each other, and Madeleine took up
where she had left off. "It's just that I could see from
the way you were looking—"

"Don't apologize," Mollie interrupted quickly, aware
that she really didn't mind talking to this sympathetic
woman about Roger. She had never before confided to
anyone about her romances—but she had never before
felt like this. "Maybe you're right, Madeleine. Maybe
I *am* in love with him."

Was she? She didn't really know.

She'd had a lot of time to think about Roger since their first meeting two weeks ago, and aside from the question of what *he* felt about *her*, Mollie had tried to be as honest about her feelings as she could be. She'd meant what she'd told Roger at lunch that day. A life without love was a dismal prospect, but it was worse to make a mistake about what you felt. Sometimes you could think you were in love when all you really felt was loneliness, or a desire to be married, or a response to someone who loved you, or just about anything except what love really was—the total acceptance of the other person with all his or her faults.

That was where she and Tim had gone wrong. He had never taken her needs seriously, and she had failed to understand that she couldn't make him do so. They'd been two people who had thought they were in love and had discovered too late that they didn't really know, or even like, each other.

Becoming aware that she had been silent for some time, Mollie's thoughts returned to the present and her friend with a start. "Anyhow," she resumed, "if I *am* in love with him, I can't imagine a single reason why I should be." To herself she added, There's his temper, his unflattering suspicions, his theories about love and women.

"Reason!" said Madeleine with a slightly derisive laugh. "What has that got to do with love? The heart has its own reasons."

Just then the sound of a child's voice came from next door. Breaking off her thread, the young mother said quickly, "It's Jean-Pierre. I must go to him." She rose to her feet. "I think my mending will hold. Be sure to rap on the wall if you ever need me." She was gone before Mollie had a chance to thank her.

Once more alone, Mollie surveyed the apartment, saw Larry's Vuittons—evidently he couldn't bring himself to refer to them as mere suitcases—and unceremoniously shoved them into a corner.

As she did so, she found herself mentally comparing Roger and Larry, and wondering wryly why she couldn't have fallen in love with the poet instead of the novelist; he was certainly more flattering to her ego. Roger had brought her nothing but anguish. No, that wasn't true, she admitted, remembering the excitement of their verbal battles, the fascination of his physical presence. Yet he had been anything but flattering. On each of the two occasions they had been together, she had ended up feeling bruised. If she could choose . . .

But one didn't choose. What had Madeleine said about the heart having reasons?

Glancing at her watch, Mollie saw that it was after one o'clock. No wonder she was hungry! Apparently unrequited love didn't ruin her appetite in the slightest. She opened the tiny refrigerator and surveyed its pitiful contents with disappointment—half a bottle of that delicious *limonade* she had discovered, the dried-out remains of a Camembert, and the stale end of a *baguette*, good only for the pigeons in the Champ-de-Mars park, which was what she had been saving it for.

Unfortunately, she wasn't in the mood for feeding pigeons. Slamming the refrigerator door shut, she tried to decide what she wanted to do. It took her only a minute. She didn't like to eat in a restaurant more than once a day, so she generally saved that for dinner, and she didn't want to have her usual picnic lunch alone because it would only make her think of the plans she and Roger had made. There seemed no alternative but to buy some food and eat in.

"Well, at least that's settled," she said to herself decisively, taking her *filet*—how handy those string shopping bags were—off its peg. I'm not going to let Roger Herrick spoil things for me, she vowed, locking the studio door and starting briskly down the stairs.

What had Ernest Hemingway called Paris? A moveable feast? Well, so far she had known only famine, but that had been her own choice, and she'd begin to do something about it this very afternoon. She'd phone some of the people she'd met last year. She knew how such things worked. She'd soon have more invitations than she could handle.

When Mollie reached rue Saint-Dominique, the shops were already beginning to put up their shutters for the afternoon closing. Hastily she bought a fresh *baguette*, two hundred grams of *pâté de campagne*, and a whole kilo—she intended to gorge herself—of luscious-looking early peaches.

Many of the shopkeepers had already begun to recognize her and she was something of a neighborhood pet, since an American woman who shopped for food, spoke French, and obviously lived in an apartment and not a hotel was a rarity.

"Bonjour, mademoiselle," said the fruit vendor as he carefully positioned the newspaper-wrapped peaches in her *filet*. "I was beginning to think we wouldn't see you today."

"I've had a busy morning," Mollie replied, mustering a smile.

The man, a kindly grandfather type, was looking at her closely. *"Ça va?"* he asked, concern in his voice. "Everything all right? Hasn't Paris been treating you well?"

"Just fine," she replied in some confusion, beating a hasty retreat. Did her misery show in her face in spite of all her good resolutions? And why should Roger Herrick, a man she barely knew, be capable of making her feel miserable, anyway? She'd better take herself in hand...

As she climbed to the second-floor studio, she passed a young delivery boy carrying an enormous bunch of lilacs, their heady scent filling the stairwell. She smiled at him, wondering which tenant was going to get such a lovely present.

"Excuse me," said the boy, "but are you Mademoiselle Mollie Paine?"

Too surprised to speak, she nodded.

"In that case, these are for you." Her arms were suddenly full of fragrant blossoms and heart-shaped green leaves. "The gentleman also asked me to give you this." He handed her a small envelope bearing her name in a handwriting she vaguely recognized.

"Thank you," said Mollie from behind the barricade of lilacs, reaching into her pocket and handing him a coin.

"*Merci, mademoiselle,*" he called back as he clattered down the stairs. "I hope they bring you luck."

Not likely, she thought as she opened her door. They were probably from Larry—his way of apologizing for all the trouble he had inadvertently caused her.

Once inside the apartment, she put the lilacs into an earthenware jug, casually tossed the note onto the couch, and began to prepare her lunch.

Well, life couldn't be all that bad since she was not only hungry but also able to positively enjoy her food. She savored more than half of the thick pâté and washed it down with several swallows of *limonade*. But she'd better be careful—if she kept on this way she'd soon be as big as Betty, back at the office.

Stopping in mid-swallow, Mollie was struck by the fact that she missed Betty. She even missed Jim Lorne. What on earth was she doing here thousands of miles from home, she wondered bitterly as she sponged off the crumbs from the folding teacart that served as a table.

The first week in Paris had been fun. She had been alone except for Odette, but not at all lonely. At least not enough to make her even think of leaving. But after one brief breakfast with Roger Herrick, and the prospect

of seeing more of him, she didn't know if she could bear
to be in the same city and *not* be with him. Should she
consider going back to New York, where she had good
friends and interesting work to keep her busy? She'd give
it another few days and see how she felt.

Meanwhile, switching on her transistor radio, she sank
into her newly mended chair and reached for the note
that had accompanied the lilacs. Might as well see what
Larry had to say for himself.

She remembered his surprising expression of sympathy for her before he'd left. He wasn't really a bad
guy, she decided. Just not quite grown up yet, and a bad
poet. She opened the letter.

"Dear Mollie," she read, "I've been a fool." She nodded in weary agreement and read on. But in the next
moment everything changed. "I ran into Larry at that
cafe we had breakfast in this morning," she read. "Of
course, he explained everything—or at least whatever
could be explained 'without impugning the honor of another lady.' He's not a bad fellow, just a rotten poet.
Actually, God must have loved rotten poets since he
made so many of them."

Mollie laughed in delight to find her own recent
thoughts not only echoed but also amplified. The expression *soul mate* came to mind—a mate for the soul.

"Can you forgive me?" the letter continued. "Please
say you do. I'll be around this evening in my by-now-
familiar sackcloth and ashes to make another attempt at
penance. Please be there." Should she? Mollie wondered.
But she knew she would.

"Larry, who seems to know the neighborhood, said
there was a good restaurant not far from the Fontaine de
Mars. I hope they know how to cook crow because I'm
prepared to eat a platterful.

"I'm staying at the Pavillon, a small place on rue
Saint-Dominique. I'll call for you at seven. If you're not
there, I'll keep coming back until you are."

It was signed "Roger."

Seven o'clock! It wasn't even three now, Mollie noted in bitter disappointment. More than four hours to go—all those wasted hours when they might have been together.

Why was she so happy? He had treated her shamefully. Immediately assumed the worst. Given her no chance to explain. Deliberately tried to wound her.

Nevertheless... the heart has reasons...

From the radio came the strains of her favorite Edith Piaf song, "La Vie en Rose."

- 5 -

MOLLIE SIGHED WITH satisfaction as she placed the very last morsel of creamy Brie on the very last piece of bread she had allotted herself. Looking up, she found Roger's dark eyes regarding her steadily. His hand approached her face, and she automatically drew back, but not before his fingertips had brushed a crumb from the corner of her mouth. She felt the touch of his hand all the way down to her toes.

"Do I frighten you?" he asked in a softly mocking voice.

Mollie had to tell herself firmly that he couldn't read her mind. Yes, he did frighten her. He had changed into a white shirt of very fine cotton batiste, tapered in the European fashion so that it fit him closely, and the force of his attraction as he sat across the small table from her was overwhelming.

When he had picked her up at the studio, he had apologized briefly for losing his temper, indicated that the subject was closed, and deliberately kept to neutral topics. Then, in the restaurant, instead of crow he had ordered a rich and fragrant *boeuf en daube* for both of them and a carafe of house wine that came from a vineyard at Barbentane where, the elderly waiter informed them, two rivers, *le* Rhone and *la* Durance, met. Perhaps this rushing together of the masculine and feminine was one reason why wines from the area were a favorite with lovers, the waiter suggested.

71

Well, lovers they were not, but Roger was certainly the most stimulating man, in every sense, Mollie had ever been with. "Roger," she began, partly to break the increasing current of physical awareness between them and partly because she was really interested in hearing what he thought, "how do you suppose Larry—"

"—ever found this place?" he finished, raising one eyebrow questioningly, as if to verify that he had guessed right.

She nodded, pleased that they were again on the same wave length. How indeed had Larry discovered such a wonderful but obscure restaurant? From the outside it looked like any other bistro, and she could tell from the other diners—mostly people from the neighborhood and a few who probably worked in the nearby embassies— that it wasn't at all an "in" place.

"I'd guess that his unnamed lady friend is responsible, wouldn't you?" Roger continued.

"That must be it," Mollie agreed. "Otherwise I can't imagine him going anywhere that doesn't have the latest jet-set seal of approval."

"I had so little faith in anything he recommended that I stopped by to check it out before suggesting we come here."

"I thought it was only women you didn't trust," Mollie teased.

Though she was becoming acutely aware that the topic of women and their trustworthiness was fraught with danger, she was surprised to see Roger stiffen.

"Even *I* don't think that women have a monopoly on untrustworthiness," he answered, with an ostentatious show of mildness.

Mollie could see that Roger was making an effort to control the irritation her question had aroused in him, but before she could comment he added, "Anyway, why so quick to come to the defense of Larry Label?"

And why was Roger so quick to take offense, Mollie

wondered. It should have been obvious that she hadn't meant her comment seriously. But if he could make a gesture toward peace, so could she, and she merely said soothingly, "You were probably right to check. It would have been awful to find ourselves in a restaurant that looked like his clothes."

Roger relaxed visibly, and after a moment they both broke into a fit of uncontrollable laughter. As their last gasps subsided, he said, "Well done!" and, reaching for her hand, kissed the inside of her wrist. "You're an extraordinary woman, Mollie," he whispered. "Some day I might even learn to control my temper for your sake."

Once more he kissed her wrist, then as though warming to the task, pulled her slightly toward him, leaned across the small table, and kissed her full on the lips. He moved so smoothly and effortlessly that Mollie's suspicious mind immediately imagined a long succession of similar scenes with similar women in similar restaurants on several continents.

"That's the second time you've done that," she said, trying to sound as if it was a fact of only statistical interest.

"I warned you back in New York that my research into the fire and ice phenomenon had barely begun."

"Have you come any closer to a conclusion?"

"Tending toward ice at the moment," he replied judiciously. "But the night is still young."

Mollie's fingers tightened unconsciously around the wine cork on the table. "I suppose in due time you'll tell me where this research is tending?"

"I thought women were supposed to be intuitive about that sort of thing," he said mockingly. "In any case the research is of the kind that requires no justification. It's an end in itself."

"And, Professor Herrick, what am *I* supposed to do while you're giving your all to science?"

"Respond as enthusiastically as you can, please."

"That will depend on whether I'm a participant or just a subject."

Roger looked troubled and then, making no attempt to disguise what he was doing, deliberately turned the conversation. "I've been meaning to ask you all evening—just who is this woman whose studio you're renting?"

Still stunned by both his kiss and his words, Mollie was almost grateful to get back onto firmer ground. "A friend of Odette Gerard's," she replied evasively. There seemed no reason to let him know that his translator had once been involved with Larry.

"Lambert made such a point of concealing her name." Roger laughed. "Not that it would have meant anything to me. Other than you, the only woman I know in Paris is my translator, Annie Dumont, and that studio doesn't seem at all her style."

Mollie played with her empty wine glass and, to get off the topic of Annie Dumont, said, "You know, Larry sent a cab driver over for his suitcases. He's staying at the Plaza-Athenée on avenue Montaigne."

"I know the place—very chichi," Roger commented with an ironic smile. "That's exactly where I would have put him if he were a character in one of my novels. Elegant but overstated. Just right for Lambert."

And that was that for Larry Lambert, Mollie thought. Observed, classified, and dismissed. As she had suspected, Roger Herrick had little tolerance for human weakness.

"Speaking of elegance," Roger continued, "I like your dress."

Mollie silently congratulated herself on having splurged on the exquisitely cut silk jersey she had bought before leaving New York. Its daringly low-cut neckline was accented by an old Victorian brooch that had belonged to her grandmother, and the supple fabric clung to her shoulders, breasts, and waist like a second skin, then floated around her like a breeze, responsive to her every movement. The dress had cost half a week's salary, but the color—a constantly shifting blend of silver, mauve, and rose for which she had no name—was as subtle and sensual as the style. She had bought both it and its companion cape with a sense of wicked pleasure.

"Thank you," she replied simply. "And that reminds me—I never really thanked you for those lilacs. I hope you don't mind my having given a few branches to Madeleine Renal."

"Is that the woman with the little boy we saw this morning?"

"Yes, and I feel so sorry for her. Her husband died in a factory fire while trying to save some of the other men, so she's been a widow since before her son was born."

Roger listened to the story of François Renal's bravery with absorbed attention, and Mollie realized that one of the reasons his books were so good was because he was always listening, always watching. He drew every one of his minor characters from life with care and accuracy.

When she had finished speaking, Roger said quietly, almost as if he were talking to himself, "You know, most people don't really find out who they are until they're confronted with a crisis. They tend to overlook everyday failures of courage, telling themselves that they'll rise to the occasion when the right moment comes along. Unfortunately," he continued grimly, as if speaking from experience, "all the little surrenders generally leave one unprepared to meet the big test."

Little surrenders. Was it their undermining effect that made Roger so determined to keep the upper hand, to win every argument? Mollie suddenly understood that he was probably harder on himself than on anyone else. And what about her? Had her big test been the decision to leave Tim? Or was it still to come? And would she have the courage to meet it when it did come? She wasn't sure. But one thing she knew without question. Roger would always have enough courage to face any situation.

"And now, Mollie," he said, "enough of this. It's time for you to give serious consideration to your duties as my tour guide. I've been to Paris many times before, of course, but I want to experience *your* Paris, the one you seem to have fallen in love with."

"What makes you think I'm in love with Paris?"

Picking up a spoon and holding it as if it were a pipe, he mimed a deep puff and, leaning back, began a Holmesian imitation that was just about perfect. "Elementary, my dear Watson. When I suggested we begin our tour, your eyes lit up with an excitement that can hardly be laid at the door of this inoffensive lovers' wine."

It was long past ten o'clock, and they were the last diners. On the tables all around them the waiters had neatly upended the chairs for the night. To make up for the fact that they had stayed so long, Roger left a tip large enough to bring a genuine smile to the weary waiter's face.

"Yes, I do love Paris," Mollie confessed as they started walking toward the river. It was true—at least it was now. Earlier that day she hadn't been sure. The city had seemed lovely but suddenly cold and distant. Tonight she again felt a part of it, in tune with all the other strolling couples whose hushed voices filled the soft spring air.

"You're not expecting a learned discussion about the height of the Eiffel Tower or the number of flying buttresses on Notre Dame, I hope," she said in a teasing voice.

"No thanks. That's everybody's—or nobody's— Paris. Besides, I know that already. Almost a thousand feet and forty-six buttresses," he announced imperturbably, adding quickly, "I told you, it's *your* Paris I want to know."

"All right, let me show you this," she said, unselfconsciously taking his hand and leading him across to the other side of avenue Rapp and pointing to one of the buildings. "How's that for art nouveau?" she asked, her pleasure at the fanciful luxuriance of the curved facade as strong as ever.

Roger considered it a moment, then shook his head. "Not for me. I see that it's good, and I can understand your liking it. After all, there's nothing similar in Philadelphia, or Chicago either, for that matter. But it's much too ornate for my taste. Good try, but you'll have to do better than that to impress me."

"Okay," she said, mock-defiantly. "Come on. I know something you won't be able to resist."

"I already know something in Paris I can't resist, Mollie," he said softly.

She pretended not to hear him and remained silent as they walked the two blocks to the Seine, still hand in hand.

"Here," she said at last. "There can't be anything more simple, more basic, more..." She searched for the right words, then just spread her arms as if to embrace the scene. Silently they leaned over the parapet and watched the lights of the bridge alongside them dance in the river. Roger put his arm around Mollie's shoulder and drew her close. She felt the warm pressure of his hand through the light jersey cape, through the thin jersey dress. She breathed in the scent of his clean masculine presence. She responded to his hard-muscled body next to hers. Her senses had never been so alive. Did she have only five, like everyone else? Could a mere five senses make her feel like this?

"... more beautiful," Roger was saying, completing her description of the scene before her. Or was he? "No guide book," he went on, placing both hands on her shoulders and turning her to face him, "could describe how lovely you look standing here—or how eager I am to explore..." His voice was husky, and his eyes never left hers as he slowly tilted her face upward.

She caught her breath and let out a soft, involuntary cry, hardly aware if the sound was a laugh or a sob. Why did she feel so unready? Was it because she didn't want to experience passion without first hearing his confession of love, because only then would she find true happiness?

Whatever the reason for her hesitation, Roger felt it and stopped when his mouth was almost on hers. Instead of kissing her, he cupped her face and his fingers slowly traced the contours of her eyes, her cheeks, her mouth. Then he released her and stepped back.

"Mollie, Mollie," he said, a faint hint of laughter in his voice. "We're neither of us children. Do you really think I've come three thousand miles to look at buildings and bridges?"

"I . . . I don't know," she said, then added inconsequentially, "I've read somewhere that when good Americans die they go to Paris."

"But I'm alive, Mollie, and not all that good," he retorted impatiently. His eyes held her as powerfully as if she were physically bound. "Can you deny that there's been something between us from the very beginning— and that you've felt it as strongly as I have? Maybe I was too abrupt that morning. But why are you fighting me now?" he whispered, his voice seductive in the soft night air.

The question only half startled her. Mollie knew he was right. There *was* something between them—a passion so strong it frightened her. But because it was *more* than physical passion for her, she wasn't ready to accept it on the terms he offered. She was no trembling young virgin, but this time she wouldn't settle for less than everything.

The sound of music came to her from across the river. Mollie turned from Roger and, looking toward the Right Bank, saw the lights of the *bateau mouche*, the boat that plied the Seine with hordes of happy tourists. She felt

Roger watching her, but remained facing the water. When he finally spoke, his voice sounded different. "Then it's back to the tour again?"

Mollie turned to him and replied quickly, "That's what you said you wanted." She was grateful for the chance to postpone a decision.

"I've said something else as well," he said evenly. "Think about it, Mollie."

Before she could answer, he shook his head, indicating that the topic was closed for now. "I see that light in your eyes again," he said with an exaggerated sigh. "What is it now?"

"The *bateau mouche...*"

He looked at her ruefully, then grabbed her hand, urging her on with gleeful exhortations as they raced over the bridge, arriving at the boat just as the gangplank was being taken up.

Standing up front and leaning against the rail, they watched as the quai slid away. Mollie was breathless.

"Are you all right?" he asked.

"I'm fine. Just a little winded."

"Too much pencil pushing, my girl. You need more strenuous exercise—and a complete change of routine."

"You're right," she agreed, knowing that she was agreeing to more than the words indicated on the surface.

He looked at her carefully, then caught his breath sharply. Once again he lowered his face to hers slowly. This time she was ready for him. He kissed her gently at first, then more insistently, and as his strong arms enfolded her she forgot her reservations and responded eagerly, matching his hunger with her own, molding her body to his. "Fire at last," she thought she heard him whisper, before all thought ended...

A gentle breeze brought the overwhelming fragrance of heliotrope to her, and Mollie slowly became aware of someone standing a few feet away, waiting, watching. She felt herself go rigid against Roger, and a second later, as he became aware of the change in her response, they were two separate people again. Reluctantly, she turned and found, as she had known she would, Odette Gerard.

"Go right ahead, *mes enfants,*" said Mollie's friend. "After all, Paris is for lovers." Her tone was detached, even melancholy.

Mollie wondered briefly if all of Paris's lovers had to put up with an interested observer peering over their shoulders, but she performed the introductions as gracefully as she could. Odette extended her hand to Roger in a manner that obviously indicated she intended him to kiss it. As Mollie watched nervously, and then incredulously, he smiled, took the hand in his, and applied his lips to it as casually as though this were an everyday occurrence in Chicago.

"Handsome," Odette said under her breath. "And well brought up."

If Roger heard, he gave no sign.

"What are you doing here, Odette?" Mollie's words came out more sharply than she had intended. They sounded like an accusation.

"Postponing the inevitable moment of sleep—or at least bed. I would like to be able to ride the *bateau mouche* more often on nights like this."

Just then they passed under the Pont Alexandre. Its richly ornamented lamps were breathtaking in the moonlight.

"Yes, the Seine is lovely tonight," Mollie said softly, taking in the separate strands of the night's beauty—the gentle lapping of the water on the near bank, the soft mist in the air, the fresh scent of damp pavement and spring flowers.

But Odette's attention had wandered, and Mollie became aware that her friend's eyes were now fixed on the boat's glassed-in restaurant area, where late diners were finishing their meals and waiters rushed about with trays piled high with pastry.

Whatever Roger may have felt about Odette's sudden intrusion on them, nothing in his manner betrayed his thoughts. He too had followed the direction of her eyes, and with swift understanding he turned to Mollie. "We never did have any dessert, Mollie, did we? I'm sure we can still get a table."

At first Mollie thought his suggestion was just a maneuver to shake Odette. She was going to protest, but Roger was already saying, "Perhaps Madame Gerard will join us." Turning to the older woman, he continued, "Mollie tells me you're a *bec-fin,* so just choosing a dessert under your guidance should be a valuable experience."

Not a hint of mockery tinged his tone, and Mollie was touched by his sensitivity toward this poor, lonely old woman.

Odette said nothing, merely briefly lowered her heavy-lidded eyes by way of assent before majestically leading the way to a table and sinking into a chair between them.

Roger ordered coffee for them all. When the waiter brought the pastries for them to make their selection, he quietly told him to just leave the tray. In the next fifteen minutes, as Mollie and Roger watched in absolute disbelief, Odette Gerard silently and methodically polished off three *religieuses*—pyramid-shaped, chocolate-covered cakes filled with chocolate custard—and a mocha éclair. Mollie had chosen a raspberry tart and Roger whatever was nearest to him—a mille-feuille, as it turned out. But neither had done more than politely taste their selections, and after Odette finished her four servings, she unceremoniously emptied their plates onto her own.

When she at last put her fork down, a contented smile wreathed her face. Nevertheless, turning to Mollie she said, "You were right not to eat this slop, but as for me I just can't bear waste." Her heavy lids closed and in the next moment she seemed to be asleep. But as Mollie and Roger exchanged smiles over her nodding head, she abruptly began to speak.

"You think me ridiculous, *n'est-ce pas?* An outlandishly dressed old woman who reeks of heliotrope, is overweight, and who insists on gorging herself with bad food at every opportunity."

Before Mollie could formulate a polite protest, Roger said easily, "Mollie and I were smiling at each other because your joining us has given the evening an unanticipated turn."

Odette looked at him intently. "Handsome, polite, *and* intelligent," she murmured, concluding some inner dialogue. She turned to Mollie, "Don't let him get away, *ma chère*. He'll give you some bad times—they always do—but when all is said and done, this one's a real male. Alas, a dying breed."

Mollie said nothing, but she was thinking of how Odette's words echoed the lyrics of an old blues recording that had been running idiotically through her head all evening: "A good man is hard to find/You always get the other kind."

"What makes you think he wants to get away, Madame Gerard?" Roger asked. "What would you say if he told you he had found what he was looking for and was perfectly content to stop the search?"

"I would say," replied the purplish mass, shaking itself so that waves of heliotrope wafted across the table, "nonsense! The male is a hunter always in search of new prey." She laughed shortly. "I should know. How you all struggle and twist away when you come upon real love. You confuse it with what you've known before, and you think of it only as a physical problem to which there is an obvious physical solution."

As though exhausted by this long speech, she again

closed her eyes and seemed almost to fall asleep.

"No doubt you know best," Roger said, a note of impatience in his voice.

"Voilà!" Odette's eyes exploded open. "A hint of contradiction even from an old frump like me and the spine of this splendid animal arches in anger! I can imagine what happens when a young and desirable woman crosses him." She turned to Mollie with a knowing laugh. "Watch out, *ma fille*. The love of a man like this can be like sharing a magnificent feast with a panther. There's no excitement to equal it, but you can end up badly mauled."

Roger's body stiffened and in the silence that followed Mollie waited—hardly knowing for what, but prepared for a storm. Oh Lord, so much had been crowded into the day! One moment she was on top of a pinnacle with the world at her feet. The next she was plunged into the depths. And then it began all over again.

To her amazement, however, a slow smile spread across Roger's face. "You're an old witch," he said to Odette, "but you're a nice old witch. I think I like you."

Odette roared with laughter, and her pleasure was so contagious that Mollie and Roger joined in.

At that moment the loudspeaker in the dining room crackled to life. "And now, *messieurs et mesdames,* we are approaching Notre Dame. Begun by Bishop Maurice de Sully in eleven sixty-three on the site of an earlier church, construction of the cathedral of Paris continued throughout the thirteenth and fourteenth centuries..."

"Let's go out on the deck for this," said Roger, rising to his feet and extending a hand to Mollie, who glanced questioningly toward Odette. But Roger was evidently determined to have some time alone with her and he continued smoothly, "I'm sure Madame Gerard will excuse us."

"Allez, les amoureux," said Odette grandly. "As for me, I'm going to take a little nap. It's good for the

digestion, and at my age that's what counts." And she snapped her observant eyes shut.

The next moment they were open again. "Just a moment, *jeune homme*," she called after Roger as he and Mollie started toward the front of the ship. "Are you the same Roger Herrick who wrote *The Weaker Sex?*"

"I'm afraid so," he answered, turning to face her. "But I'm beginning to think it was only an apprentice work. After all, I still hadn't met... you."

Odette acknowledged the compliment as no more than her due by nodding her head regally. "Life has some surprises for you," she said sleepily. "But the book shows talent and an ability to learn. Women are a great deal more—and less—complicated than you suspect. Perhaps *la petite*"—she gestured toward Mollie—"can help set you right."

"If you'll excuse us," Roger replied bluntly, "I'd like her to take on the assignment as soon as possible."

On deck they watched in silence as the illuminated facade of Notre Dame loomed up out of the darkness. It was so beautiful that a shiver ran through Mollie.

"Cold?" Roger asked, drawing her close to him.

She shook her head. "No, that was a thrill of pleasure. Really, I'm as sentimental as a schoolgirl."

"You may feel like a schoolgirl," he said, suddenly holding her at arm's length and letting his eyes travel appreciatively down the length of her body, "but right now you look like a sliver of moonlight."

"It's the dress," she answered, surprisingly shy about the compliment.

From the loudspeaker, the voice was saying, "... and the parapet was added in the fourteenth century. The facade, badly damaged during the revolution, was restored in the nineteenth century by Viollet-le-duc..."

"I hate to admit it, but I don't really care about all these facts," Mollie said guiltily. "I just want to feel it all inside me."

"Your instincts are absolutely right," Roger approved. "The response to beauty should always take the form of direct action rather than talk." And as though to demonstrate his point he drew her close to his side again, this time encircling her under her cape and holding her so that her breasts rested lightly on his arm.

Mollie's immediate response was almost a reflex action. She stiffened in surprise and drew away. But it was too late. They'd made contact, ignited the spark—and the slight intervening space she had created between them by her movement seemed cold and empty. Of her own volition she closed that space again, holding his hand imprisoned in hers.

As Mollie looked up into Roger's face, the moon which had until that moment been shining brightly slid behind a cloud, and his features became shrouded in darkness. Something similar had happened only that morning, when he had first appeared outside her door and the hallway *minuterie* had gone out. First you see him, then you don't, she remembered thinking. Now she feared that maybe it would always be like that.

But if she was temporarily deprived of the sight of him, her other senses seemed by contrast to have become all the more sharp. Only his presence beside her mattered—the sense of his body next to hers, the feeling that wherever he touched her he claimed her as his. As if reading her mind, he began to enlarge that territory. His hand, which for a time had accepted its imprisonment, freed itself effortlessly and began to roam, its touch so light that though his fingers barely skimmed her, they seemed to penetrate the thin fabric of her dress and set her on fire.

Only seconds had elapsed since Roger had first put his arm around her—seconds during which the still night remained undisturbed except by the thumping of her own heart, challenging her, daring her to respond to what life offered—even if the terms were still to be decided.

As if in reply to that challenge, Mollie moved for the first time, faced Roger squarely, and deliberately placed her hands on the back of his neck, bringing his face down to hers. His kiss was long and deep, filling her with a wild longing that soon matched his. Now her hands explored too, learning for the first time the lithe power of his neck, his shoulders, his strong back, his chest. When her hand reached his heart, she felt it beating fiercely, in rhythm with her own, and with a small cry of joy she broke their kiss, brought her face down, and burrowed into his chest as if to merge even more closely with that heart. As she moved, he pursued, his lips following the curve of her face till they found the little hollow near her earlobe, and then the earlobe itself.

Time stopped, and then Mollie heard through the stillness of the night the nearby sound of a bell ringing out the hours. Ten, eleven, twelve—the hour when Cinderella's robe turned to tatters and her coach and six to a pumpkin drawn by six gray mice. Poor Cinderella, she thought sympathetically, but aloud, her cheek against his shirt, she only said dreamily, "I wonder where those bells are coming from." Her voice sounded strange to her, as if it were traveling from a great distance.

"Saint-Julien-le-Pauvre," Roger answered softly, his warm breath in her ear.

"How can you tell?" she asked, so astonished that she raised her face to his. "Paris is filled with small churches. There's one on practically every corner. How can you recognize the bells of any one of them?"

"I happen to know those particular bells very well," he replied.

His words conjured up a vision of him in Paris, and not alone. Suddenly a cold chill seemed to have come between her flesh and his. Her robe had indeed turned to tatters and her coach to a pumpkin.

She drew back and faced him. Now the moon was shining brightly and she could see his features clearly.

He was smiling ambiguously, as though remembering something, and a flash of jealousy exploded inside her.

He brought her to his side again and held her close, but Mollie felt herself receding from him at a dizzying pace.

"How often have you been here in Paris?" she asked, struggling to keep her voice casual.

"Often. I spent a couple of summers here during college, and since then I've come for my . . . for my books."

Mollie tried to shift her position slightly, but Roger imperiously pushed her head down on his shoulder again. Putting me in my place, she thought sadly, and struggled to free herself so that she could talk. "It shows. I'll bet Odette was impressed with the fluency of your French."

"Damn Odette!" he exploded, reluctantly recognizing Mollie's change of mood and loosening his hold on her. "However, since you brought it up, let me tell you, young woman, that my French *is* very good, though I'll probably never get anyone over here to agree," he added ruefully. "Actually, Annie Dumont has been a great help with it."

"Oh?" said Mollie, in what she hoped was a neutral tone. She failed to meet his eyes.

"She's a good teacher," Roger continued, "but God help me when I make a mistake." Once more he seemed to be smiling at some secret memory. "Last time we were talking about Les Halles, the wonderful old marketplace they've torn down to make way for that monstrous new Forum, and I made an incorrect liaison. She nearly snapped my head off. 'R-r-really, R-r-roger, it's time you learned how to make your liaisons correctly. The *h* is aspirated.'"

Mollie tried to laugh but found she couldn't. She could, in fact, do nothing but wonder if Roger had indeed made "an incorrect liaison," and at the thought she became aware of a huge constriction in the area of her heart. What was this Annie Dumont really like? Dare

she ask? Could she make the question sound casual
enough?

"...a regular hellcat," Roger was saying. "Claws
bared in a minute and ready to scratch my eyes out for
an aspirated *h*."

Mollie found herself remembering something Odette
had said one day. *"Ma chère,* it's only in bed that one
really learns a language. As for me, I speak English,
Italian, Spanish, and alas, only a little Russian."

So Annie was a hellcat. And what happened when a
hellcat and a panther got together?

Moving silently along the velvet surface of the black
river, the boat had gone beyond Notre Dame. The night
was still as lovely as ever, but somehow it was now all
wasted on Mollie. She was unhappy, and once again a
shiver ran through her.

"Another thrill of pleasure?"

She straightened up. "I'm afraid I *am* cold now,
Roger. Do you mind if we go inside?"

"Won't my jacket help?"

Not if your arms don't, she thought. She shook her
head. "I think we'd better go in. Besides, we really
shouldn't abandon Odette like this."

"For God's sake, can't you forget about Odette for
a moment?" Roger protested. But he saw that Mollie was
determined. "All right," he added. "But something's
happened. What is it?"

"I don't know," she whispered, unable to tell him.
"I just don't know."

He looked at her sharply but asked no further questions.

Silently they returned to the dining room, where they
found Odette busily demolishing yet another pastry.

"This one was worse than the others," she said with
a guilty blush. "Abominable!"

They all laughed, but only Odette seemed happy.

- *6* -

BY THE TIME the boat returned to its dock, Roger and Odette had become great friends. To Mollie's surprise, this man who had been so quick to display his hair-trigger temper at the slightest hint of disagreement or criticism from her seemed to enjoy the jibes the older woman directed his way, often in a French too salty and colloquial for Mollie to fully understand.

At Roger's suggestion, they had finished off the evening with a well-chilled bottle of Veuve Cliquot champagne, and had shared so much fun and laughter—in which even Mollie joined—that she found it something of a letdown when the three of them descended from the *bateau mouche* and stood on the deserted quai. She was wondering what to do about seeing Odette home when Roger said decisively, "It's late, and Mollie and I still have a few things to settle. I wonder, Odette, if you would allow me to send you home in a cab?"

"That would be very kind of you," said the old French-woman, her eyes boldly taking in the two young people with a smile that made Mollie blush.

Roger seemed not to notice. Stepping into the street, he hailed the first cab that came along. As he paid the driver to take Odette back to rue Monge, Mollie noticed that the cab—an antique that looked as if it might have been one of the taxis that rushed French reinforcements to the battle of the Marne in World War I—had a little decal of the Russian imperial eagle pasted on the windshield.

When Roger opened the taxi door for her, Odette swiftly leaned over, kissed him on the cheek and then, with a comically regal nod to them both, stepped swiftly inside. Before the door had completely closed behind her, they heard the older woman exclaim in happy surprise, "Why, Sergei!"

The driver cried, "Odette!" and then with a roar and a splutter the cab drew away. Mollie and Roger glanced at each other with blank looks. "Sounds like Odette's met an old friend," Roger said after a moment as they watched the cab disappear.

"How nice," Mollie replied approvingly. "I've been feeling sorry for her all evening. Funny. She's so full of life that I hadn't noticed before how completely alone she is." Mollie slipped her arm comfortably into his, and they started walking along the Seine toward the Palais de Chaillot. "Or perhaps," she continued after a moment, "I'd gotten to the point of accepting that kind of loneliness as part and parcel of the human condition, as inevitable as death and taxes."

Without commenting, Roger brought his arm against his side, simultaneously imprisoning and caressing her own. His wordless response was full of understanding. Even the sound of their footsteps echoing along the deserted quai was not a forlorn sound because they were together.

"I wouldn't feel too sorry for her." He laughed, deliberately lightening the mood. "Odette's a tough old bird. In her heyday she must have been quite a beauty, and I doubt if she spent many evenings knitting by the fireside. In fact, I suspect that the only purls she ever knew came from Cartier."

Mollie laughed. "That's a perfectly awful pun, and I'm afraid that as your editor I can't allow it. Besides, it's a heartless thing to say."

"Not at all," he protested. "I'm merely being realistic and objective. Odette sees life as a luscious pastry that's of no use to anyone unless it's consumed."

"Maybe," Mollie conceded hesitantly. "But if she was as gluttonous about life as you seem to think, then she must be all the more despairing now."

"You mean," said Roger, "that patisserie is no substitute for passion? How right you are!" And as though to emphasize his point, he took her into his arms and lowered his lips to hers. After a series of light, quick kisses, he released her and announced lazily. "Raspberry. Definitely raspberry."

Suddenly his moonlight-flooded face clouded with doubt. "Unless . . ." His lips once more sought hers, his arms resting lightly upon her hips. As both of them began to breathe more rapidly, Roger broke away. Like a deep-sea diver coming up for air, he proclaimed judiciously, "Unless it's gooseberry. There's a tartness there I can't quite identify. *Could* it be gooseberry?" He had begun to lower his head to hers again, but she stepped agilely from his embrace.

"Once they reminded you of fire and ice," she said, gently pummeling her fists against his strong chest. "That was much more poetic." They were both laughing now.

"Mollie, I love your laugh. Promise me you'll laugh more often."

"Like most women, I only ask for an opportunity," she replied. Again she linked her arm with his and soon they emerged from the shadows of the quai into the bright lights of the place de Warsovie.

"And I, like most men, am only seeking an opportunity." He said it lightly enough, but for some reason even here, with the dazzling lights of the *place* behind them as they began to cross the Pont d'Iéna, Mollie felt the shadow of a menace beneath his words. It wasn't what he had said but what he seemed to imply that bothered her, and she had to force herself to reply gaily,

"Alas, men and women don't always view opportunity in the same manner."

"There's only one way *to* see it. As something to be seized—and held and held and held." He suited his actions to his words. And held and held and held. Yes, that was what she wanted. To be held.

They were standing in the middle of the bridge now. Beneath it a barge cut swiftly and silently through the Seine with a barely audible but melodious swish. Facing them on the Left Bank, the dark shape of the Eiffel Tower soared into the starry night, standing guardian to the vast Champ-de-Mars park behind it.

Mollie felt lost in a dream. Real life wasn't like this. It wasn't boat rides on the Seine, kisses in the moonlight, a romantic play presented against a Parisian backdrop. Real life was filled with regrets and hidden disappointments. She had only to think of Odette, or of Betty back in New York, back in the real world and not in the magic of this night, to know how often patisserie had to substitute for passion. She wouldn't let it happen to her. Roger was right. Happiness must be seized.

Almost without her knowing it, she increased her hold on him. Something never before fully awakened stirred in her like the memory of an imagined event. This time her mouth sought his. His lips felt warm and firm beneath her own, and moved with an urgency that was very real.

But when she finally drew away, his expression remained unchanged and he didn't say anything. It was almost as if they hadn't kissed at all. As if they really were only imaginary lovers. Only the Champ-de-Mars through which they were now strolling like disembodied shadows was real.

Yet Roger's arm was now resting lightly on her shoulder and she was conscious of its weight, its warmth. He had to be real, and so was she, or she could not have felt that weight and warmth. And the tourists who, even at this hour, stood around the base of the tower were also real, all of them. She imagined them whispering, "I love you" in every language of the world. *Te quiero; Ich liebe dich; ti amo . . .*

She laughed, but not with amusement. It wasn't a pleasant sound even to her own ears, and she knew Roger must hear the difference.

"I preferred the other laugh," he said, frowning. "There's something ambiguous about this one. Anyway, what's so funny?"

"Do you really want to know?"

"Well, I don't happen to have a penny with me, but would a fifty-centime piece do?"

"Sir, I'm not to be bought." She laughed again. "Or at least not for foreign coin." Mollie paused. "But I'll be generous."

"I had hoped you would be," he replied, simulating a leer.

"Generosity can take different forms," she replied. "Men are unbelievably single-minded."

"We have to be—the competition is so enormous. I know a Swede who is something of an amateur naturalist, and he once explained to me that that's why the peacock was given all those beautiful feathers."

"You mean so that he can spread his gorgeous tail and just wait for the drab peahen to be dazzled?"

"Something like that. But of course not all hens are drab. And obviously the peacock sees something in them, or the breed would die out."

"You and your friend may be right, but speaking for the hens, I must say that this grand plan of nature seems a little impersonal."

He was silent. Mollie waited for a moment and then went on. "Do you still want to know about that ambiguous laugh?"

"Of course." His tone was serious.

"I was suddenly struck by the fact that I've been on an emotional roller coaster ever since I met you yesterday morning." The editor in her winced at the ordinariness of her metaphor. It was the worst of clichés, but it exactly described what she had been feeling, and Mollie prayed that Roger wouldn't pretend not to know what she was talking about.

They had stopped walking and now stood facing each other. His reply, when it finally came, was not at all reassuring. "My advice to you, assuming you're interested in advice, is to ride with it. Yes, ride with it and take advantage of every opportunity the high points offer."

They began moving forward again, and just before they reached the traverse that would lead them on to the rue de Grenelle, they came upon a group of people standing around an accordionist who was softly playing Mollie's favorite song—"La Vie en Rose." Some of the younger couples were waltzing on the lawn to the sound of the music. They looked like people in a dream, silently listening or dancing in the moonlight.

"And speaking of opportunities . . ." said Roger, opening his arms in an invitation to waltz.

Ride with it, he had said. She would try. Kicking off her shoes, she once again surrendered to the bliss of being held in those strong arms with her head resting on his shoulder. She was happily lost in the moment. The spring grass felt soft under her stockinged feet. When he took her in his arms, she saw life as a rosy dream.

He was holding her lightly but firmly, and she moved her head from his shoulder to his chest. Once more she breathed in his manly scent. Every moment seemed to last forever.

Finally the song came to an end. The music stopped with a last long chord. The accordionist acknowledged the applause and drifted away with some friends. And Mollie and Roger turned out of the park. Yes, she decided, she would ride with it. She would trust her instincts . . .

"I'll be busy at my publisher, Flammarion, most of tomorrow," Roger was saying casually, "but I should be finished about six. Do you know the Café Cluny on the boul' Mich? We can meet there and plan the rest of the evening over a drink."

His voice held an almost peremptory tone, an unthinking, arrogant assumption that henceforth her time would be at his disposal. The thought disturbed her, and although she told herself she was being childish and difficult—after all, wasn't that just what she wanted, to spend as much time as possible with Roger?—it didn't seem to help.

Perhaps it was irrational of her, but she found his confidence irritating. It was almost as if he felt that he had put himself out all evening to woo and win Mollie by being nice to Odette, being sympathetic with what he must see as Mollie's insane changes of mood, and now she *must* be convinced, and all he had to do was to harvest the prize and tell the lady what would be expected of her in the future.

Mollie knew she was not being fair. What she wanted from Roger was probably more than he could give her. And if she were really honest with herself, she'd acknowledge that she was tormented by a jealousy inspired by a woman she had never seen, a woman whose real relationship to Roger she knew nothing about.

With difficulty she kept herself from shaking free of his touch, and when they reached her front door she found herself saying, despite what she thought she had decided and more firmly than she would have believed possible only ten minutes before, "I won't invite you up. I'm much too tired."

She expected, even hoped, that he would protest—and indeed he seemed about to do so—but instead, without her knowing exactly how it happened, she was in his arms again. His lips were pressing down on hers, his tongue skillfully finding its way into her mouth, insisting that she receive him, his hands confidently mapping the contours of her body. All her quibbles and doubts were consumed by the desire he sparked. . . . Then, as suddenly as he had begun, he stopped.

Smiling, his voice caustic, he released her and, reaching behind her, pressed the *minuterie* inside the door. "I've told you. Don't play games with me, Mollie. I've had more experience with them than you have."

She waited, but he said nothing more, and Mollie was half convinced that he had read her mind and was punishing her for what he had found there. One minute she had been silently objecting to his assumption that she was his for the taking. The next minute he had proved that she was. And the minute after that she was dismissed. Shaken, she realized she didn't want to be left alone, but she found she couldn't say anything. He was right. She had been playing a game, and now she wanted to tell him that she wasn't really tired, that she was ready to "ride with the high," that she had just given way to the green-eyed monster. But the moment had passed. He stood there, ironic and detached, and there seemed no way to undo what she had done.

As she climbed the stairs, he called after her, "Six o'clock at the Cluny."

She let herself into the studio, trying to pretend it didn't really matter. But when she had closed her own door, heard the hall light go out, and felt the vibration of the heavy front door slamming shut, she allowed herself the luxury of shedding the first tears for a man since the day she and Tim had decided to split up.

The next morning Mollie indulged herself by sleeping later than usual. She had spent a restless night—what had been left of it—and it was well past nine-thirty before she stretched a lazy arm from between the sheets and switched on her transistor radio, now permanentl: tuned to France-Culture.

As often happened, she had missed the news and weather and come in on a lecture, this one about the glories of Mont Saint-Michel and the dangers of its sudden tides to unwary tourists who ventured upon the sands surrounding the little island. Turning the radio up a little, she went into the bathroom to shower, hoping that the information would at least help improve her French. Her mental capacity, she had decided after her erratic behavior last night, must be beyond repair.

The voice on the radio buzzed on, unreeling endless facts and figures and reminding Mollie of the tour lecture on the boat. Inevitably that thought brought back memories of sensual pleasure that made her melt inside . . . and she also found herself thinking about Roger's sensitivity toward Odette. He had given her a glimpse of a side of him she had suspected but never before been allowed to see. Yes, there was no doubt that the hours they had spent together had drawn them closer. But something she couldn't understand prevented her from fully relaxing in his presence. Was this unknown something in her or in him?

Nothing was clear. He said he wanted to know her, but did he really? Was he interested in her as a person or as just another sexual conquest? If he really wanted to know her, why did he so often respond to her emotional overtures with a cynical remark? "Ride with the highs"; "seize the opportunity"—that wasn't what she wanted to hear, even though his touch could make her forget what she wanted. And why, *why*, was he often so inexplicably quick to anger? When all was said and done, wasn't he basically more comfortable with an inaccurate preconception of her than with the truth?

Oh, part of it was her fault, she acknowledged, frowning into the mirror as she brushed her teeth. For example, why had she become so upset at the casual mention of the mysterious Annie Dumont?

There! She was doing it again. Why mysterious?

Roger wasn't hiding any secrets about Annie. He had, in fact, said quite clearly that she was his translator in France, that she had helped him improve his French, and that she had something of a temper. Yet Mollie had to admit that the mere mention of Annie's name had been enough to set up a barrier between them—and it was she herself who had erected it.

Roger obviously had no idea that this same Annie Dumont was the owner of the studio Mollie was renting... or that she was the lady whose reputation Larry Lambert seemed intermittently eager to protect.

No, there was no mystery about Annie Dumont. She was evidently a talented translator who was furthering her career by collecting literary lions—or at least cubs— under the pretense that her work required close collaboration with her authors. Nothing strange about that. Mollie had often met her equivalent in New York publishing circles.

But how closely had Annie Dumont *collaborated* with Roger Herrick? Mollie wondered—and decided it was really none of her business. After all, he was thirty-five, unmarried. She remembered guiltily her pleasure at discovering that particular fact when she had looked him up in *American Authors* the very day she had met him. And he had undoubtedly known many women in his life. She had no right to feel possessive. But despite what she told herself, Mollie realized that that was exactly what she did indeed feel. Was she, with all her pride and independence, to prove Roger right after all? Was *every* woman in love either a piranha or a jellyfish?

No, she promised herself, she'd never act like the stereotypical women in Roger's novels. She couldn't help how she felt, but she could certainly control the way she behaved. Or could she? That was obviously the trouble, Mollie told herself sternly. When she was with Roger she lost control.

Becoming impatient with herself and her brooding,

Mollie turned to the more immediate problem of deciding what to wear. She surveyed the contents of her armoire and gave way for a moment to a gnawing sense of dissatisfaction. Then she began to laugh. No, clothes were not her real problem, though it might be fun to spend the afternoon shopping anyway.

Shaking off her moodiness, she dressed in a pleated blue-and-white-checked skirt, a soft blue bow blouse, and sling-back navy flats. With her navy blazer, she'd be set for the whole day and wouldn't have to return to the studio before meeting Roger that evening.

Meanwhile she put coffee on and decided not to be lazy about breakfast. She'd run down and get some croissants.

She had to wait several minutes in the long line of housewives out doing their morning shopping. When it was finally Mollie's turn she got a friendly *bonjour* from Madame Sylvain, the baker's buxom wife, paid for two croissants which the woman twirled into a cocoon of tissue paper, and started back, half running. She hoped the coffee hadn't boiled over.

As she arrived at the door of the studio, she heard the, to her, amazing sound of what she recognized as a top pop tune coming from her radio. It was called "L'Almighty Dollar." "The almighty dollar, the almighty dollar/They live in luxury, we in squalor," lamented the singer.

Heads will roll tonight at France-Culture, Mollie thought, laughing to herself at the idea of such frivolity emanating from that solemn radio station.

But as she inserted her key, Mollie realized that the door was open. Inside, sitting on the still unmade bed and removing his shoes, was a bushy-bearded blond giant. He seemed surprised to see her.

"How did you get in here?" Mollie demanded, incautiously closing the door behind her. But she was sure she already knew the answer.

Digging into his pocket, the big man grinned and held

up a familiar key. "And a good thing too," he said in French with an unusual accent. "Your coffee was boiling over."

"Oh no!" Mollie cried, sinking into the chair. "Not again!"

"No harm done. I got it in the nick of time," said the giant, obviously thinking she meant the coffee. "Where's Annie?"

"Annie doesn't live here anymore." Mollie sighed wearily. The line was beginning to sound like a refrain.

All the joy drained from the stranger's face. "I knew my good luck wouldn't hold," he said softly. "No, not bloody likely." Then, regaining his good humor, he added philosophically, "Oh well, I guess nothing lasts forever." He reached for the hem of his basque shirt, then calmly began pulling it over his head.

"Stop that!" Mollie said sharply. "I'm afraid you can't stay, Monsieur . . . Monsieur . . ."

"Bjorn," he volunteered, putting his shirt back on. "Bjorn Pompidou. And your name?"

"Mollie Paine. I'm renting the place until the end of May, and I have no idea where you can find Mademoiselle Dumont."

They had been speaking in French, but now he suddenly switched to English. "You're an American, aren't you?"

She nodded.

"Well," he said soothingly, "that's all right then. We're both strangers in a strange land. I'm Swedish, or at any rate half Swedish. When my mother was a young girl," he went on conversationally, "she visited Paris and was much taken with a dark-haired man who introduced himself as Monsieur Pompidou. Unfortunately she never saw him again after their informal wedding night."

The story didn't seem to embarrass him or make him think less of his mother. He stretched and yawned, then continued, "Strangers in a strange land, as I was saying. If we don't help each other, who will?"

His voice trailed off; he seemed to be dozing there, perched precariously on the edge of Mollie's bed.

"What have you got in mind?" she asked, raising her voice in an effort to awaken him. For some reason she wasn't at all afraid—maybe because Bjorn Pompidou looked like a big friendly bear.

He opened his eyes reluctantly. "First of all some breakfast," he answered, significantly eyeing the tissue-wrapped croissants she was still holding in her hands.

"Okay so far," said Mollie, bustling over to the stove. She wondered for a moment if she was crazy, if she ought to rap on the wall to call Madeleine. But Bjorn seemed harmless enough.

"And then," Bjorn continued, once again reaching for the hem of his shirt, "a bed to sleep in."

"Oh no!" Mollie cried again, whirling around with the coffee pot in her hand, not sure whether to pour him a cup or use the pot as a weapon.

"Relax! Relax!" He looked genuinely perplexed at her response, but Mollie remained on her guard. "Look," he went on in a reasonable tone, "I crossed over to the continent from Malmö more than twenty-four hours ago, and I've been sitting up on crowded trains ever since. I'm dead for sleep and I don't have the price of a hotel room."

"I'm afraid I can't help you with that," said Mollie stonily. Nevertheless she poured him some coffee and gave him one of her croissants, which he dispatched so quickly that she decided he must have eaten as little as he had slept. Refilling his cup, she sighed regretfully and pushed the remaining croissant toward him.

"Thanks, Mollie. Look, I'll make a deal with you."

"No deals, Mr. Pompidou."

"Think before you say no. How do you plan to get

me out of here? Of course you could call for help, but how would you explain the presence of a half-naked man in your room?"

"It would be easier than you think," she retorted, brooding about all the keys to the apartment that must be scattered among various men in foreign lands. Immediately she realized that he had misunderstood, and she regretted her words. "You were saying?..." she said quickly.

Looking at her closely, Bjorn evidently decided that whatever he'd been thinking had been a mistake. "Just let me have this bed to myself for a few hours, though you're welcome to join me if you want. And when you come back I'll be gone. I promise. I'll slip my key back underneath the door and you need never see me again."

"That part, at least, sounds promising," she answered, softening somewhat. It was difficult to dislike him.

He laughed happily. "I'm actually a very nice guy when I'm fully awake."

"I'll take your word for it," she said. "Okay. I must be crazy, but all right—it's a deal. It's almost eleven o'clock now. I'll take what I need for the day, and you can have the place until seven. Eight hours ought to put you back on your feet."

"Bless you!" he replied, and immediately slid between the sheets."

"I won't still find you here when I get back?" Mollie asked anxiously.

"Not bloody likely."

He was apparently asleep before she went out the door and quietly locked it behind her. She wondered where, without money, he would spend the night—but that wasn't her problem. Besides, an attractive man like that would undoubtedly find something.

On balance, Mollie decided she rather liked Bjorn Pompidou and might have been much taken with him under other circumstances. He was certainly a decided improvement over Larry Lambert. Annie Dumont must think so too, because he couldn't be just another literary notch in her belt. He looked more like someone who sailed primitive rafts across the Pacific Ocean than an author, famous or otherwise. In any case he was certainly a persuasive fellow. Here she was, an exile from her own apartment because of a man she hardly knew.

Well, she didn't really mind. The whole day stretched before her, and she was glad to have it to herself. There was lots she could do, and much to think about. For instance, why did just knowing that she and Roger would be together that evening charge her with such energy? Everything was up in the air between them and it was both their faults. He had been a bit too offhand about her. She had been too suspicious of him. Worst of all, from the way she had behaved last night he probably thought she was nothing but a tease. Cards on the table; let's not play games . . . he was right.

Since she still hadn't had breakfast, Mollie stopped in the bakery for two more croissants. Madame Sylvain looked surprised but didn't comment. Discretion, thy name is France, Mollie thought as she walked along rue de Grenelle, munching hungrily.

At the esplanade in front of the Invalides, she briefly considered going in to see Napoleon's tomb, then decided it was much too nice a day for anything as gloomy as a mausoleum. Napoleon could wait.

When she reached rue de Rennes, Mollie turned left, and after detouring up and down a few narrow sidestreets, finally ended up at the old Saint-Germain-des-Prés church. She loved the area—every block presented a different feast for the eyes, and she had already spent an afternoon wandering in and out of the many galleries and craft shops. She also remembered seeing some boutiques in which she was sure she could pick up at least a couple of shirts—the prints were charming and even the cheaper ones were beautifully cut. There really was something to this notion of the "French touch," she thought not for the first time.

By two-thirty she gave up. There certainly were a lot of boutiques, and shirts too. But either the color wasn't right, or they didn't have her size, or she just wasn't in the mood.

All at once she realized she was famished. It was too late to be served in most restaurants, so she settled for an omelet and a cup of coffee on the open terrace of a nearby brasserie, feeling very Parisian as she sat watching the world go by. But the sky was rapidly clouding over, and suddenly it began to rain. This was the first day the weather hadn't been perfect. Mollie had neither a raincoat nor umbrella with her, there were still more than two hours before meeting Roger, and she couldn't even take a taxi home. Luckily, a theater just across the boulevard was showing an American film she had missed. She decided to go in even though the show had already begun. Again feeling like a true native, she slipped a *pourboire* into the waiting hand of the usher who had showed her to her seat, then settled back, wondering once again at the strange custom of tipping in theaters.

The film was a comedy, and at many points Mollie found herself the only one laughing. Somehow the ploddingly faithful subtitles seemed invariably to miss the comic point, which made her begin to brood about the problems of translation.

Was Annie Dumont able to do any better than this in turning Roger's uncompromisingly American prose into French? Mollie assumed she was, since Roger, a perfectionist about his work, had seemed satisfied with the results. But then, she told herself wryly, Annie Dumont had the advantage of close collaboration with the author.

Mollie closed her eyes for a moment, and the next thing she knew the house lights were on and the audience was moving toward the exits.

It was a little after five. The air was soft and mild after the rain, but the day was beginning to feel long. She was eager to be with Roger, to tell him that she'd been foolish last night...

By five-thirty she had bought a copy of *Le Monde* and was seated with her newspaper at a table on the terrace of the Café Cluny. By six o'clock the tables began filling rapidly. A half hour later there was not another table to be had, and Roger Herrick had still not made an appearance.

Seeing Mollie alone, a portly middle-aged man offered to buy her another white wine, but with a frozen smile she explained that she was expecting someone.

"It's hard to believe anyone would keep a pretty woman like you waiting," he protested.

She replied sweetly. "Yet it's true." Her French was improving even if her temper wasn't. Perhaps, she thought, remembering how Odette had acquired her language skills, it might someday be as smooth as Roger's. But, she wasn't about to start with *this* monsieur!

The man looked at her for another moment, decided the situation was hopeless, and with a regretful shrug moved off in search of other prey.

With increasing irritation, Mollie checked her watch. Roger was now forty-five minutes late and she was beginning to feel she'd taken root. About to pay her check and leave, she suddenly saw him half a block away striding down the boulevard Saint-Michel from the direction of rue Racine, where she knew the Flammarion offices were located. At his side walked a petite, elegant woman dressed all in black and white, with a dramatic black rain cape closed only at the throat. She seemed in no great hurry. In fact, just before they reached the corner, the woman clutched Roger's arms and made him stop to look at something in a bookstore window.

As the woman talked on, punctuating her remarks with animated gestures, Roger's eyes swept the tables of the cafe. Spotting Mollie, he gave an ambiguous shrug that he might have meant as an apology. Shrugs said a lot in this town, but nothing very clearly, Mollie decided.

"I'm sorry to be so late," Roger said when he finally arrived at her table. He remained standing, his capable-looking hands resting lightly on the back of a chair. "I was just about to leave when Annie said she had to make a couple of phone calls. The building was deserted by that time, so she asked me to wait."

The woman with him had stopped at another table to talk to a young man with an interesting if somewhat too intense face framed by a *collier*—the trim beard that seemed as much standard equipment in the Latin Quarter as faded blue jeans. "In case you're curious," Roger continued, following the direction of Mollie's eyes, "that's Pierre Midi the poet she's talking to." Mollie *was* interested, but not in the young poet, though he served as an excuse for keeping her eyes fastened on Annie Dumont, the woman whose fascinating past had been so strangely shaping Mollie's present.

"He's a kind of French version of our Larry." Roger's tone was disdainful. "His poems are currently the rage of the Quarter, especially a bad-tempered little item called 'L'Almighty Dollar' that somebody's set to music." He laughed. "If it weren't so unconsciously funny, it would be offensive."

"I've heard it . . . many times, unfortunately," Mollie said, interested in spite of herself. "The rhymes have all the subtlety of a sledgehammer."

"I guess nobody loves a rich uncle," Roger said as he sat down. "Seriously, Mollie, I want to apol—"

But Mollie never heard the rest of that sentence. "Why, R-r-roger, she's absolutely charming. You gave me no idea."

Mollie looked up and found herself staring into the artfully made up face of Annie Dumont. "Do give me a chair, Roger. I'm dead on my feet." As she would have

to be, thought Mollie, having noticed the high-heeled
black shoes from across the street. Admittedly they set
the other woman's legs off to splendid advantage. She
had to keep herself from looking down at her own "tourist
flats."

Roger silently offered Annie his chair, then reached
for the empty one next to it that Annie had ignored.

"Thank you," she murmured softly, at the same time
resting a manicured hand—the nails were long and blood-
red—on his arm.

"I'm Annie Dumont," said the woman, reaching an
almost lethal-looking talon across the table to Mollie. It
slid from her grasp like a cold fish.

"Mollie Paine," she answered briefly.

She turned to Roger, but his face was impassive,
detached. She did notice, however, that his shopping trip
had been more successful than hers. He was wearing the
same chinos, but his jacket was of dark green linen; his
light green-and-tan-striped shirt was open at the neck and
worn without a tie. He managed, Mollie noted with approval, to look dressed for anything without looking
"dressed" at all.

"I know, I know," gushed la Dumont. "Roger has
spoken so highly of you that I was almost intimidated."
She paused, then added, "But how could I have thought
that a lovely young thing like you would be intimidating?"

The words seemed friendly enough, but given the fact
that Annie was probably only a year or two older than
she, Mollie caught another implied message—no competition here. The sense of relief Annie conveyed was
practically the only real thing about her.

Mollie smiled noncommittally but said nothing. She
was afraid to trust her voice lest it betray her irritation
at this elaborate show of condescension.

"Now you mustn't scold Roger for keeping you waiting." Annie gave him a soft pat on the arm. "You see,

I absolutely *had* to make some telephone calls, and since the building was empty by that time, he gallantly insisted on remaining with me." She shook her head in exaggerated admiration. "You Americans, you're absolutely from another century."

"I thought France was the country of old world charm," said Mollie.

"Gone, my dear. Absolutely gone with the wind." Annie, who had been speaking English, brought the latter phrase out proudly, obviously content with her command of colloquial American.

She seemed prepared to be contradicted, but Mollie only said, "Perhaps you're right."

Her tone made it quite clear that she didn't take Annie's observations very seriously, and the French woman again looked at Mollie very carefully before turning to Roger. "Aren't you going to offer me a drink, Roger? I'm absolutely dehydrated after our strenuous tussle."

"Annie's been looking at the most recent version of *A Woman in Love.*" Roger explained to Mollie. "Says she loves it just the way it is and doesn't want me to change a word."

A mocking gleam shone in his eyes, but Mollie wasn't sure who was being mocked.

"Pas un mot!" said la Dumont emphatically, looking straight at Roger. "Not a word," she repeated in English. "Oh, I admit that your portrayal of women in the first half is unflattering, but we're all so masochistic that we'll love it." She turned to Mollie. "Don't you agree?"

Mollie sensed a trap and sought to avoid it. She was still hoping—with a growing fear that her hopes were doomed to disappointment—to have that wonderful evening she'd promised herself with Roger. But if she began to criticize his book, things were sure to go from bad to worse. All authors, she had learned, were like new mothers, sensitive to even a hint of criticism about their offspring. And Roger, as she had also already learned, was one of the touchiest.

"I'm sure Mr. Herrick expects to appeal to his male readers too," she finally said coolly.

"Doesn't she call you Roger?" Annie asked. "I thought you knew each other a great deal better than that."

Roger couldn't ignore this direct question, but he looked somewhat put out. "Mollie's merely on her company manners," he said shortly.

"You're annoyed with me for making you late," said Annie, in a tone dripping with phony apology. This time the manicured claw came to rest on Roger's hand.

"I'm not annoyed," he replied, "but it occurs to me we must be keeping you. You said something about an appointment you were already late for."

"And so I am." Annie glanced at the ridiculously small watch that circled her fine wrist. "But that dreadful Pierre Midi is sitting there. He wanted to have dinner with me, but I told him—it was the only way I could escape— that I was having dinner with you two."

"Why didn't you just tell him you had a previous appointment?" Roger asked.

"It's too complicated to explain," she replied quickly. "In any case"—she looked at Mollie appealingly—"you understand, don't you? If he sees us going our separate ways now, he'll know I lied to him."

Annie seemed more concerned with having her lie *discovered* than with lying, and when Mollie looked over at Pierre Midi's table, she saw that he was in animated conversation with a friend and quite oblivious of Annie Dumont's very existence.

"Oh, I understand, all right," Mollie said pointedly. Changing the subject, she turned to Roger. "Another one's shown up," she said.

"Hold on a minute, Mollie. If we're going to stay on, let's have those drinks." And having ascertained what they wanted, Roger gave the waiter the order before turning back to face her. "Another what?"

"Another man with a key."

Annie Dumont had been following their exchange but now she looked blank, so Roger explained politely. "Mollie's rented a small studio on rue de Grenelle, and it's beginning to look as though every male visitor to this town has been given a key by the former occupant." He turned back to Mollie too quickly to see the look of alarm on Annie's face. "What was this one like?"

"A Swede. Quite nice, but dead broke. I left him sleeping off a twenty-four-hour train trip after he promised to clear out by seven."

Roger glowered. "You mean he's in your bed?"

Mollie laughed at him, and after a while he smiled back. "You can't believe how exhausted he was"—she looked at her watch—"and I'm sure he's gone by now. Anyway, you seem to forget that it's no more my bed than a bed in a hotel would be."

"True, but maybe you ought to have the lock changed," Roger said thoughtfully.

"Oh, I don't know," Mollie replied airily. "I think such unexpected guests lend a certain excitement to living there. Besides, if I do that, just think of how disappointed my landlady's admirers will be. Don't you agree?" She directed her question to Annie, who now seemed preoccupied.

"Where did you say you were staying?" Annie asked Mollie slowly.

"Rue de Grenelle."

La Dumont took this in, thought for a moment, then said with apparent amusement, "How did you happen to end up there? It's so far from things."

Mollie hesitated for the merest fraction of a second before replying evenly, "A friend of mine, Odette Gerard, found the place for me."

- 7 -

ANNIE DUMONT'S FACE gave no hint of whatever inner turmoil she may have been experiencing, but Mollie, who was observing her closely, sensed the tension behind her self-control, and for a moment she was ashamed of herself. It was cruel and pointless to taunt this woman when she had absolutely no intention of betraying her secret.

Suddenly Annie began rummaging energetically through her bag. From where Mollie was sitting, she saw her start to fish out a pack of cigarettes and then, evidently changing her mind, drop it back into the voluminous depths.

"Damn," said Annie, "I'm out of cigarettes." She looked at Mollie. "I know Roger doesn't smoke, but would it be too much to hope that you might have some?"

"I'm afraid I don't smoke either," Mollie replied.

"No, of course you wouldn't. So many of you American women have no minor vices."

Her voice was challenging, and it seemed to Mollie that Annie was skating on thin ice. For a moment she admired her nerve and then she realized that the Frenchwoman was deliberately trying to goad her into saying something she might regret. Any comment she made about Annie's generosity with her keys would cast Mollie in the role of a gossip and talebearer, and in all probability that was exactly what Roger expected a woman to be.

111

No doubt to his way of thinking, only a man was capable of respecting the privacy of another person's life. Remembering the almost adolescent eagerness with which Larry had overcome his scruples on this score, Mollie smiled.

"I amuse you?" Annie said sharply.

Mollie was again startled by her tone but replied quietly, "No, I'm afraid I don't understand what I'm supposed to make of that last comment. But in any case I was thinking of something completely different."

"Roger," said Annie, turning to him brusquely, "do help me."

For the past few minutes he had been watching the two of them attentively, and Mollie could see that he was perfectly aware of the tension in the air.

"What is it you have in mind, Annie?" he asked circumspectly.

"Oh, you needn't worry. It's nothing more onerous than running across Saint-Michel to that *tabac* on the corner. I must have a cigarette."

"How unimaginative, Annie," he murmured with a knowing smile, but he rose, made a slight apologetic bow to Mollie, and threaded his way smoothly through the closely packed tables.

"Always the perfect gentleman," said Annie ironically as the two women watched him.

"Yes," Mollie agreed, "though not always so even-tempered." And she wondered why this man, so often quick to fly off the handle where she was concerned, now behaved with perfect equanimity when he was obviously being sent off on a fool's errand.

Annie smiled. Clearly indifferent to what Roger might think on his return, she again reached into her bag, removed a cigarette, and lit it. Taking a deep puff, she slowly released a cloud of smoke into the air and said abruptly, "Why didn't you tell him?"

Mollie saw no reason to pretend that she hadn't under-

stood. "What business is it of mine—or of his?" she
probed. She waited, wondering what Annie might reveal.
"And besides, since you seemed so eager for him to have
the information, I thought it would be best coming from
you."

Studying her thoughtfully, Annie smiled. "I've underestimated you," she said, then gave a surprising little
chuckle. "I suppose that's what comes of working so
closely on Roger's books. He's such a convincing writer
that I've almost come to believe his oversimplification
of our complicated sex."

Annie's comment was an open invitation to join her
in a feminine conspiracy against Roger, and Mollie rejected this gambit too. "I thought you completely agreed
with his point of view. You said you didn't want so much
as a word changed."

"Luckily I'm a translator, not an editor," Annie replied. "I don't have to agree or disagree with Roger's
ideas. My job—and I do it well—is to put what he says
into French. I want to give readers here the impression
that everything in that book was originally thought and
written in their own language." She paused and took
another puff on her cigarette. "It's not easy, but contact
with an... intelligence... as fine as Roger's has its own
rewards."

"Is that why you feel it necessary to work so closely
with him?"

Annie laughed. "Not exactly... but then, you must
understand my dedication. After all, isn't it the same as
yours?"

Before Mollie could answer, Roger returned and
wordlessly handed Annie a pack of cigarettes.

"Stupid of me," she said as she met his eyes. "As
soon as you left I found a crumpled pack at the bottom
of my bag." She held the outsized soft leather pouch up
for him to see. "I really should use a smaller one, or one
with compartments. It's a wonder I can find anything

once it disappears into this. I can't seem to hold on to keys, for instance, and I've had to make Lord knows how many sets." She dropped the bag into her lap and leaned back with an exaggerated sigh.

Mollie gasped at her daring and found herself reluctantly admiring this elegant woman's performance—for that's what it was—even if she couldn't understand the point of it. But then, an actress is always onstage, with or without a reason.

Mollie didn't really think that was the answer. After a few moments she thought she understood Annie Dumont's intention more clearly. The performance wasn't being staged solely for Roger's benefit but partly for her own. "See," Annie seemed to be saying, "I can get away with anything, because this man, in spite of his obvious superiority, is essentially not one whit more perceptive than other men. He's so taken up with the performance that he neither sees nor suspects a thing."

Mollie wondered if Annie was right. Certainly Roger seemed to be watching the other woman with fascination, but there was a moment—and it passed so quickly that Mollie wasn't sure if it had really happened or if she had imagined it—when she could have sworn she had seen his lips form the word *piranha*. What he said aloud, however, was, "I don't mean to hurry you, Annie, but aren't you going to be late for that appointment you mentioned earlier?"

"Why? What time is it?"

"Well after seven-thirty," he replied, checking an old-fashioned watch he had drawn from his fob pocket.

"Where did you get that?" Annie, evidently totally indifferent to the question of a previous appointment, leaned over and plucked the watch from Roger's hands.

"Careful with that, now. It was my grandfather's, and I suspect *his* grandfather's before that."

"I didn't know you had a grandfather," Annie said

pertly. "You Americans all seem to have sprung from the earth only the day before—full-grown."

"Well," Roger replied imperturbably, refusing to be drawn, "now you see how wrong you can be about me." A mischievous gleam shone in his eyes as he added, "The fact is, Annie, that I had two grandfathers, as well as two grandmothers, and all of them just as real as if they were French." As Annie arched her eyebrows in surprise at some underlying message in his tone, he reclaimed the watch and carefully tucked it back into his pocket.

"I didn't think you would be so prickly, Roger," Annie said thoughtfully. Then she turned to Mollie and said, "This seems to be my day for underestimating people." Her tone changed and she added in a decisive manner, "Since it's so late, I don't think I'll keep that appointment after all. I'm sure he . . . they . . . must have grown tired of waiting and gone on to dinner without me."

As though struck by a sudden inspiration, she then turned away from Mollie and addressed herself to Roger. "Look, why don't we spend the evening ironing out one or two of those translation problems?"

His reply was immediate. "I'm afraid that's impossible, Annie. Mollie and I have other plans."

"Oh I'm sure Mollie would understand." Annie turned to face her again. "You see, a successful French edition of this new book would guarantee its sale everywhere on the continent. You do understand how important that is, don't you?"

Before Mollie could reply, Roger said firmly, "Mollie might understand, but I'm not about to change my plans—not even for royalties piling up in dependable Swiss francs. You see," he added, "Mollie and I have some unfinished business too, and I've been looking forward to concluding it all day long."

Annie was more surprised, and considerably less

pleased, by this statement than Mollie, but she knew how
to cut her losses and she recovered quickly. "In that case
I mustn't keep you. You have my number," she said as
she prepared to leave. "Call me and we'll set up something." With a curt nod to Mollie, she swooped up her
bag and left.

Mollie and Roger followed her progress between the
tables which were now beginning to empty, and watched
as she stopped to talk once more to Pierre Midi. He
seemed reluctant to comply with whatever she wanted,
but he finally shrugged dramatically, lurched unsteadily
to his feet, and followed her onto the boulevard Saint-
Germain, where they were soon lost from sight.

Roger laughed, and Mollie turned to him inquiringly.
"I don't think Pierre Midi is going to be an amusing
companion for Annie. She told me earlier in the day,"
he explained, "that he's going through an agonizing reap-
praisal."

"Why? I thought that dreadful 'L'Almighty Dollar'
was very successful."

"That's just it." His laugh was wickedly irresistible,
and Mollie smiled in response. "You see," Roger continued, "it seems that those treacherous Americans have
taken the song to their hearts and paid him a bundle for
the rights. He's become so rich that he's now an object
of suspicion throughout the Latin Quarter."

"Poor Pierre," Mollie said tartly, relishing the story.

"Poor is hardly the word for him." Roger grinned.
"Do you realize that he's probably made almost as much
money with that one song as I have with four novels?"

"Maybe you should try being anti-wealth instead of
anti-women," Mollie said, half seriously.

Roger had been leaning back on the rear legs of his
chair but now sat sharply up to the table. "Not now,
Mollie, please. I'm so hungry I could eat a bear. Let's
go somewhere and feed the inner man before I start
behaving like an animal. My father gets impossible when

he's not fed on schedule, and my mother insists I'm just like him."

"In that case . . ." Mollie replied, rising in mock haste.

They automatically turned down the boulevard Saint-Michel and began to walk toward the river, momentarily forgetting their hunger in the pleasure of being part of the bustling crowd. They talked and walked and walked and talked some more, and Roger seemed in no hurry to do anything else.

"What are they like?" Mollie asked abruptly, surprising herself when the question broke like a bubble on the surface of her thoughts.

"Who?"

"Your parents."

"The kids?" He looked down at her startled face and explained, "That's what my brother, Ross, calls them. They're incredible. Devoted to each other after almost forty years. They were delighted to be alone together again when Ross and I were finally out of the house. Why?"

They were crossing the boulevard, maneuvering through the heavy traffic, and Mollie was able to temporarily ignore the question. Finally they turned into rue de la Huchette, a narrow brick-paved street closed to automobile traffic and thronged with strolling couples who, like themselves, were consulting the menus posted outside the many restaurants on either side. Eventually they chose a North African place, where they were served a spicy beef couscous, which they gratefully washed down with a dry Algerian wine.

The restaurant was so noisy and bustling that they could hardly hear each other. They ended by eating in companionable silence, watching the other diners. Though they had enjoyed the meal, they were not sorry to leave, and continuing along the street they soon found themselves back at the river in front of the windows of Shakespeare and Company, an American-owned bookstore.

Several copies of *The Weaker Sex* were prominently displayed in the window.

"My shame for all the world to see," Roger groaned.

"Why shame?" Mollie asked. "I thought it was quite interesting."

"Don't be condescending. I like you better when you're uncompromising." His face darkened ominously. "You were quite precise in your earlier criticism of it."

"Well, you yourself recently called it an apprentice work," she replied slowly, as though testing unsure and dangerous ground. He looked at her keenly and she added in a rush, "It's what I've said before. The picture you offered was incomplete."

"Are we back to that? I thought I'd explained that every woman you've read about in my books is a portrayal of some woman I've known in my life." He spoke slowly and with careful emphasis. "Nothing you can say will change that fact."

Mollie was afraid that another discussion of his ideas about women would only lead to another quarrel, but there was no way to skirt the topic. It was too central to their relationship. Strange—they seemed to be able to agree about so much else, even to finish each other's thoughts and sentences.

"I'm not so much interested in changing facts as in challenging their interpretation," Mollie said. Without waiting for a response, she continued, "A while ago you asked me why I was curious about what your parents were like."

"Yes, and I noticed that you avoided answering me."

"I wasn't being devious," she replied slowly. "It's just that I wasn't really sure of the answer. But now it seems to me that it might have some bearing on what we're talking about. What we've *been* talking about ever since that morning in Jim's office."

"I don't see any connection, but I'll keep an open

mind, so go ahead. Do your damnedest, Ms. District Attorney."

Mollie refused to rise to the bait. "Are you like your father?"

"I suspect you're changing the subject, but the answer is yes. And yes, the old man can be pretty testy, with or without his dinner."

"Does your mother handle him by being either a Jenny or an Amanda?"

"Why, neither, of course. How else could they have survived as a couple for forty years?" His voice trailed off and he was silent for a moment, absorbing what he had just heard himself say. "I see what you're getting at."

Mollie remained discreetly silent.

"You witch," he whispered. Completely indifferent to the jostling crowd around them, he leaned down and said softly, "There's only one way to stop that pretty, pedagogical mouth of yours." He drew her into a crushing embrace, his mouth insistent against her own.

Mollie was breathless when he let her go. "You don't fight fair," she said, shaken.

"I fight to win."

She smiled but said nothing. It wasn't the first time he'd used a kiss to stop a discussion that was becoming awkward. Still, this was their first "editorial conference" that hadn't ended in an actual quarrel. Maybe they were making progress.

A very young American couple had just emerged from the bookstore, and as they passed, Mollie and Roger saw that the man was holding a copy of *The Weaker Sex*. "I don't know, David," the young woman was saying spiritedly, "but it seems to me that the title is ironic. Which *is* the weaker sex?"

"Maybe you're right, Jeanie," the man answered, sliding his arm around her waist. "As a matter of fact," he added, "just now I'm sure you're right."

Mollie looked at Roger, wondering if he was aware of any parallels, but he obviously wasn't going to comment. Instead, he reached into his pocket and pulled out a street map of Paris. "Here, you're supposed to be my tour guide, remember?"

"But I don't need a map," she protested. "You forget that I've spent a whole week poking around, and I certainly know how to get from here to wherever I decide to take you."

"I'm sure you do," he replied, pointedly ambiguous. "All right then—take me, I'm yours."

They both laughed, but Mollie's laugh sounded hollow to her. Would he ever be hers?

When they arrived at the bridge leading to the Ile de la Cité, they crossed and walked slowly past the familiar facade of Notre Dame. Then, taking a narrow street on the north side, they stopped across from the famous rose window, under which ran an open gallery of lacy stonework.

"Too bad we can't see it from the inside with the light streaming through," said Roger. "At first it's just an abstract blaze of color, and then slowly you begin to see all those Old Testament stories come through."

"Here, here," objected Mollie. "I thought *I* was supposed to be giving this tour."

"You are. I'm following you all the way." He put his arm around her and drew her close. "And I've found parts of it fascinating."

"I hoped you might like it," said Mollie.

Just then her eye was caught by a sign that read AU CENTRE POMPIDOU.

"Next stop," she announced, stepping out of his embrace so that she could think more clearly, "is the Centre Pompidou, better known locally as the Beaubourg."

"Just when I was getting to like it here." Roger sighed.

"You're really inexorable, aren't you? Don't you know the museum will be closed at this hour?"

"Yes," Mollie agreed, "but that's when the area is most interesting."

They crossed another little bridge to the Right Bank. The streets here were quiet and their footsteps echoed in the hushed night. Mollie was aware of how quickly they had fallen into a pace comfortable for both of them. "I was here the other night," she said. "There's a great open area in front of the museum and the whole place was like a scene out of the Middle Ages—absolutely swarming with magicians, musicians, sword swallowers, mimes, acrobats, tumblers, and strong men."

"I thought you didn't particularly approve of strong men," Roger commented, a hint of the old arrogance creeping back into his voice.

"Then you thought wrong," Mollie protested. "In fact, I've always hoped I might someday link up with a *really* strong man."

"You mean someone who'd whack you over the head with his club, grab you by the hair, drag you back to his cave, and never let you out again?"

"That wasn't the kind of strength I had in mind," she answered. "A man who has to keep a woman under lock and key is a man who is depending on the strength of prison bars, not his own. Most women are quite clear about the difference between brute force and real strength."

"Brute force is what's behind all strength. Why won't women acknowledge the fact?"

His voice was impatient, but the words came out so quickly that Mollie knew she was hearing an almost automatic response. They had come to the end of the quiet street they had been following, and she was saved from the need to reply by the fact that the Beaubourg had suddenly reared up before them. The semicircular, inclined area leading to its doors was completely surrounded by cafes, boutiques, souvenir shops, bookstores—and people everywhere.

The museum itself looked like a petroleum refinery at night. Ablaze with light, its open construction was framed by a geometric pattern of colored pipes and exposed exterior escalators.

"I've seen pictures of this, of course, but the reality is even stranger than I'd imagined. It's not what one generally expects a museum to look like," Roger mused.

"No," Mollie agreed, "but then it was planned to be less intimidating than the Louvre or traditional museums, and it seems to work."

They toured the various impromptu entertainments taking place in the open space fronting the museum, stopping for a long time at a puppet show. In addition to the various couples linked arm in arm who seemed to make up the majority of Paris's population—or was it just that Mollie was particularly aware of them?—there were many family groups. The children squealed with delight at Punch's antics. Nearby stood a fire-eater filling the dark night air with eerie bursts of flame. He too had a crowd around him.

"What's going on over there?" asked Roger, holding Mollie's elbow firmly so that they wouldn't be separated and urging her toward one of the smaller, quieter groups.

A man was entertaining a dozen or so people with nothing more elaborate than some squares of black paper and a pair of scissors.

"Why, he's making silhouette portraits," Mollie said with delight. "I didn't think anybody still knew how to do that sort of thing."

"Shall we give the man a chance to see what he can do with us?" Without waiting for her to answer, Roger asked the man if he could do couples.

"Mais oui, monsieur," the man answered with a laugh. "Couples only present problems for each other."

A few minutes later he produced a very recognizable likeness of the two of them in profile. When the black cutout was mounted in a small cardboard frame, it was as if they had been captured for all eternity, and Mollie felt it was more *them* than if someone had taken a snapshot. She put the silhouette carefully in her bag.

As Roger was paying the man, Mollie stepped back from the group surrounding the silhouette maker and brushed accidently against someone wearing a camera around his neck. Turning to apologize, she found herself staring into the delighted and amazed face of her early morning Swedish visitor.

"Why, it's *la belle Americaine,* my good angel!" he shouted.

"Bjorn! What are you doing here?" she asked in some confusion.

"Where else should a Pompidou be?" He roared at his own joke. "I can't thank you enough. I feel like a new man after a few hours of sleep."

The blond giant had engulfed her in his arms, lifted her off the ground, and was whirling her around in a grateful hug when, over his shoulder, Mollie saw Roger striding toward them, an unreadable expression on his face.

- *8* -

FINALLY MÀNAGING TO free herself from Bjorn's enthusiastic embrace, Mollie apprehensively reached for his arm and turned him around to face Roger, whose reaction she was still trying to decode. "Bjorn..." she began. But Bjorn had freed himself from Mollie and the two men were already rushing at each other.

When he was very close, Roger stopped short and stepped back as though in fear. "Oh, no," he said, "you're not catching *me* in that bear hug."

But it was too late. To Mollie's amazement both men—one dark, tall, and lithe, the other a sturdy blond giant—were soon locked in what looked like a life and death struggle. After a few moments she lized with relief that the incoherent shouts coming from them were happy ones, and that all the strenuous back thumping was friendly in intent.

When things quieted down somewhat, Mollie heard Roger say, "Bjorn! Until I saw that familiar Hasselblad, I wasn't even sure it was you. I can hardly recognize you with all that face fuzz."

"Just a protective layer," the colossus replied with a laugh. "You forget how cold winters in Sweden can be."

"Not bloody likely," replied Roger, imitating what Mollie already recognized as Bjorn's favorite English phrase. "There are parts of me that still haven't thawed out since our last meeting. How long ago was it?"

125

"Three years. I'm not bloody likely to forget what a fool I made of myself." Bjorn turned to Mollie. "I arranged for us to go skiing one day, thinking I could take Roger down a peg or two, but as soon as we got up into the mountains he literally skiied circles around me. How was I to know he'd gone to school in New England and been on the college team?" His laughter exploded once more, then he sobered enough to continue. "As a matter of fact I broke a couple of ribs trying to keep up, and Roger had the devil's own time getting me back to the chalet again."

"You two know each other?" Mollie asked foolishly, still unable to connect these two strands of her life.

"Mollie," Roger said gravely, "I'd like you to meet Bjorn Pompidou, an old friend and the best nature photographer in Sweden, if not the world."

"But we've already met." The big Swede was shouting so exuberantly that people nearby turned around to watch. "She's my good angel. She saved my life when I arrived this morning, dead tired and without a franc in my pocket. But how do you two know each other?"

Roger hesitated. "Mollie's my editor in New York."

"Still scribbling away, are you," replied Bjorn disapprovingly. "All those silly words you people write! They never get at the truth anyway. You'd do better to get out in the fresh air more often."

"You're absolutely right," Roger quickly agreed. "Anytime you're up to another skiing trip..."

"Not bloody likely! Find some other victim."

"Come on now, you're exaggerating. It wasn't as bad as all that."

Instead of answering, Bjorn turned to Mollie. "Watch out for this one," he said knowingly. "One minute he seems as meek as a lamb and the next..." He left the sentence unfinished.

"So I've discovered," Mollie answered wryly.

Bjorn inspected her closely, then looked carefully at

Roger and back again at Mollie. "You and Roger? . . ." he began, a light breaking over his face.

"No," said Roger quickly. "Mollie's my editor and a candidate for the role of mentor." He regarded her intently. "Did I get that right?"

Mollie felt chilly all of a sudden and put her hands deep into her jacket pockets. Was he trying to protect her, or was he specifying the limits of their relationship. Instead of answering Roger, she turned to Bjorn. "Did you find anything to eat at the studio?"

"I'm afraid I just about cleaned out that toy refrigerator of yours," he replied, looking stricken. "Some leftover pâté, peaches, and every last crumb of the *baguette*. There's nothing left but a little mustard." He paused and then his face assumed its usual joyous expression. "But that was hours ago. I'm still broke and I'm still hungry. And above all, I'm still thirsty."

All three of them immediately turned toward one of the smaller cafes ringing the plaza. Though it had become much cooler, Mollie pleaded that it was too lovely to go indoors, and they chose a table in a protected corner of the semienclosed terrace.

Bjorn ordered two ham sandwiches and a large beer, and then immediately began peeling one of the hard-boiled eggs stacked in a little wire stand on the table. Buttoning her blazer, Mollie decided on a hot chocolate. Roger asked for a *fine à l'eau* and excused himself. In some puzzlement they watched him leave the cafe and disappear around the corner.

"Where's he off to?" asked Bjorn.

Mollie shrugged. "Your guess is as good as mine." It wouldn't have surprised her if he had simply chosen this moment to walk out of her life.

"I suppose his royalties are still good enough so he can pay for all this?" Bjorn asked Mollie as an after-thought. "I won't have a sou until I stop by the *Paris-Match* office tomorrow and get them to cough up for a photo series I did. It won't be much, but I'll manage."

A frank smile broke over his face—perhaps at the appearance of his sandwiches. "The truth is I left on the spur of the moment and didn't have time to get much money together." He looked at Mollie slyly. "As you know, I also didn't expect to have to pay for a hotel."

Roger, suddenly reappearing, heard Bjorn's last words. "Mollie told me all about the big Swede she found in the studio this morning," he said, beginning to undo a small package.

"Did she also tell you that I took not only her breakfast but her bed as well?" Bjorn regarded Mollie with sudden sympathy. "I shouldn't laugh about turning you out of your own place like that. I guess you've been wandering about ever since, though I can't say you look any the worse for wear," he added cheerfully.

"She will if she doesn't put this on," Roger said, handing Mollie something white and fluffy.

"What are you talking about?" she asked. "And what's—oh, it's a sweater! But Roger—"

"Put it on before you turn purple," he interrupted shortly. "They didn't have many sweaters. It's evidently bikini season for women. But this looked like the blue one you were wearing in New York so I thought it would do. Put it on, I said."

"I heard what you said, Roger, but I can't let you—"

"Come on, Mollie, don't be foolish. It's not a diamond necklace or a mink coat. You're not being bought or compromised or whatever the word is these days."

"That's not the point."

"Look," he said impatiently, "the point is that if you don't put on this sweater under your jacket, Bjorn will be forced to give you his very disreputable turtleneck or I'll be forced to give you my jacket—and you'll be responsible for giving one of us pneumonia."

"You're right, O master of logic," Mollie finally

agreed. "Thank you." She had to admit that the white mohair sweater—a much better one then her blue angora back home—made all the difference.

"Thank God that's settled," said Roger fervently. Savoring a sip of his brandy and water, he turned to Bjorn. "Now let's get back to you. What made you suddenly decide you had to be in Paris?"

Bjorn's enormous hand came down and slapped his broad thigh. "You're going to laugh, Roger. I know your opinion of women—though God knows I've never been able to read one of your books!" He stopped as if reminded of something. "I have to admit, however, that somebody whose opinion I respect about these things told me they're quite brilliant."

"Well"—Roger smiled—"I'm not surprised you can be fooled. You never were much of a reader."

Mollie watched the two men. They were completely different, but their affection and respect for each other was obvious. Beneath their superficial differences lay shared values and genuine liking. Why was such a relationship so much easier between two men than between a man and a woman, she wondered.

"So it was a woman who made you leave Stockholm in such a hurry," Roger was saying thoughtfully. "But what makes you so sure I'd find that laughable? How do you know it wasn't a woman who made me suddenly leave New York? Is that so hard to believe?"

Becoming aware of how revealing this statement might be, he quickly added, as if making a joke, "Who knows? It might even be the same woman."

Bjorn looked amazed by the whole idea. "You? You put yourself out for a woman? Not bloody likely! Why should you? They fall at your feet without your doing that." He put up his hand to stop Roger's protest and continued, "As for the rest of your nonsense, we're not attracted to the same type—at least not as a general rule." He smiled at Mollie.

Busy with her own thoughts, she acknowledged his somewhat heavy-handed compliment with a slight nod. Had Bjorn and Roger both come to Paris on the same search? And what would happen to their friendship if it turned out that they were indeed interested in the same woman? Bjorn had quite clearly come for Annie Dumont, and for all she knew, Roger might have too. But he'd come directly to her own apartment, Mollie reminded herself fiercely.

"Let me get this straight," Roger was saying. "You met this woman only once, but you know you love her and you're sure she loves you. She's not where you thought she'd be, but you're sure you'll find her. Is that really what you're telling me?"

Bjorn nodded his agreement.

"You're an incredible romantic, Bjorn, and I think I *may* very well laugh," Roger concluded. His voice expressed an equal mixture of dismay, disbelief—and something else Mollie couldn't identify.

"On the contrary," said the blond giant equably. "I'm a realist. I don't ask too much of people and that way I'm never disappointed. *You,* my friend, are the romantic. You're constantly searching for your ideal, and when you don't find her you're bitter and cynical. . . . Isn't that so?"

He addressed the last question to Mollie, but she was glad he didn't wait for an answer. "And besides, why be so bloody American about it?" he continued, turning back to Roger. "I saw her one time, two times, a hundred times! What do statistics have to do with love? Dante saw his Beatrice only once, yet he loved her all his life and even chose her for his guide through paradise."

Mollie thought of the day she and Roger had first met. What Bjorn was saying made perfect sense—that's the way it had happened to her, immediately and forever. But she could understand why Roger looked so startled.

He wasn't the type to see a woman once and choose her
as his guide to paradise.

When Roger finally spoke it was about something
quite different. "I thought you never read anything," he
said slowly, "and now I find you're an admirer of Dante."

Bjorn's fair complexion reddened as he explained
apologetically, "You know, once I spent several interminable weeks in the hospital while some broken ribs
mended. One day I asked a nurse's aide if she could find
me anything funny to read. She came back with *The
Divine Comedy*."

Mollie laughed as heartily as the two men, but she
felt that the conversation was between them. They had
practically forgotten her presence. She found to her surprise that she didn't mind, that in some peculiar way just
being with them—with Roger especially, of course—
was enough. The bond between them was so strong that
she felt included in everything he did, everything he
thought.

As so often happened, her thoughts turned back to the
past, to that time when her first chance at happiness had
ended in bitterness and recrimination. Once again she
began reviewing those events for some clue to their meaning. What had gone wrong?

Tim had originally been far from unkind. If he had
turned nasty in those final days, it was because she had
shown an absolute inability to adjust to his notion of
what a wife should be. As for accepting her as she was,
that had obviously been impossible for him. He wanted
a doll wife to fit into his house of doll Victorian furniture.
No, she would never again become seriously involved
with a man who wasn't sure enough of himself to let her
be herself.

Something she heard must have penetrated her con-
sciousness because she was suddenly aware that Roger
was still caught up in a discussion of Bjorn's attitude

toward women and love. It was almost as if he were working something out for himself. Instinctively Mollie knew that his conclusions would be important for both of them. Bjorn's next question confirmed this feeling.

"Seriously, Roger," Bjorn was asking, "what is it you want from women? Isn't it enough that they take us out of ourselves? That they're good to look at, pleasant to be with, nice to go out with or come back to?"

"No!" Roger answered with surprising passion. "I'm looking for a woman who is all the things you describe — and much more. A woman who is content to breathe her own air and not be constantly trying to rob me of mine. A woman who is sure enough of her own worth so that she isn't always trying to incorporate me to fill up her own emptiness. A woman to walk beside me, not one who has to pull or be pulled."

As Mollie watched, Bjorn's face became troubled. "Ah, my Puritan friend, you're even more romantic than I thought." His good-natured features relaxed once more into a smile. "As for me, I'm content to take them as they are. When I was a boy, I substituted a dream of women for the reality. Afterward I learned to accept the reality in place of an impossible dream." He dropped his eyes and began eating his second sandwich.

"*Is* it an impossible dream?" asked Roger, turning to Mollie.

She hesitated. "I don't know," she answered finally, her eyes locking with his. "But if it is, I share it. What you're searching for in a woman, I'm hoping to find in a man."

Again she seemed to have surprised him, but before he could say anything, Bjorn rose abruptly to his feet, blocking Roger's view. "My God, there she is! I told you I'd find her!" He crowed with triumph as he pointed to a crowd gathered around the human flame-thrower, by the light of whose fiery breath Mollie thought she recognized Annie Dumont. Her arm was linked casually through that of a man—was it Pierre Midi?—who seemed a little the worse for drink.

"Look, Roger," Bjorn said hastily, "with any luck I won't have to use it, but let me have the key to your hotel room so I can be sure of a bed for the night just in case. You shouldn't be needing yours," he added, winking at Mollie.

Roger extended the key. "I'm at the Pavillon on rue Saint-Dominique," he said dryly. "There's a couch in my room if you need it."

"She couldn't be so heartless." Bjorn laughed, snatching the key and dashing into the crowd. Mollie wasn't certain who he meant.

For a while she and Roger sat together in complete silence. Finally, Roger said, almost to himself, "Couldn't she, though!" Without consulting her, he rose, called the waiter, and paid the check. "Shall we go?"

Mollie, still silent, also rose.

"Want a cab?"

She shook her head. "I'd rather walk."

"Are you sure? We're a long way from home."

"I know," she said, her heart skipping a beat at his use of the word *home*. "But I love the city at night. Please..."

He nodded and they started off, this time along the Right Bank, past the Louvre, where a clock was striking midnight inside an invisible inner court, alongside the deserted Tuilerie gardens, across the brilliantly lit place de la Concorde. At Pont Alexandre they crossed back to the Left Bank and, using the Eiffel Tower as a landmark, made their way to rue de Grenelle. From time to time they passed other silent couples, but none as silent as they were. An unanswered question hung in the air, like a barrier between them. *"She couldn't be so cruel." "Couldn't she, though!"*

It was well after one o'clock when they arrived at Mollie's door. Roger stopped, let go of her hand, and looked at her. She understood. She had made her decision last night when she had finally acknowledged what she had known all along. She loved Roger Herrick, and she would follow her heart honestly. Silently she took his hand again and led him into the building.

Once inside the studio, she nervously switched on the architect's lamp on the low, broad shelf serving as a desk. Still silent, her back still toward him, she removed her jacket and the white sweater, throwing them on the chair, then went to the bag she had tossed on the bed, took out the silhouette portrait, and propped it on a shelf.

Roger remained still and silent.

"Why?" he finally asked roughly, after what seemed an eternity.

Because my darling, she thought, *I can hold out against the whole world but not against my love for you.*

Turning, she saw him, rigid and unsmiling, standing with his back against the closed door.

"A woman's prerogative," she said, echoing one of their earlier conversations.

"Are you sure?" he insisted. "I want you desperately, and have from the first moment I saw you, but you must come freely." His words lingered in the silent room. "Have you thought it through?"

The upper part of his body was in shadow and once again Mollie couldn't see his face at a moment when she most needed to. "I'm trying not to think at all," she said finally.

Her words seemed to satisfy him. As he moved from the door, coming slowly closer, she saw that his eyes were blazing, his face alive with joy and desire. He had never looked more attractive, more vital. But how was she to interpret his smile? What was it? Triumph at her acquiescence?

"Yes," he said gruffly. "Desire is a great obstacle to thought."

Before she could answer she was in his arms, his lips

lightly brushing her eyes, her cheeks, her earlobes, the nape of her neck. As he kissed her, Mollie's hands echoed the movements of his mouth, fingering his eyes, cheeks, ears, the shape of his head, and the tangle of his hair. His body pressed against hers, hard, urgent, unyielding, taut with self-control. At first Mollie wanted their embrace to never end. This moment was delight enough, she thought, savoring the sensations his touch aroused. But when, with one hand still holding her closely, he pulled apart the bow tie of her blouse and began to undo the buttons, she knew those kisses weren't enough, knew she wanted more, knew she wanted all of him.

A passion rose in her like none she had ever known before. The intensity of her response was frightening. She could never pretend she had been seduced—her desire matched his. And as she realized this she momentarily broke their embrace. Quietly and deliberately, not once removing her eyes from his, she began to emulate his actions, slipping off his jacket and opening first the top button of his shirt and then the others, one by one, slowly circling her free hand over the ever-increasing expanse of bare, muscular chest exposed to her touch.

Catching his breath, he matched her button for button, caress for caress, lingering lovingly over first one breast and then the other. At some point Mollie's eyes closed again, the better to feel every touch given and received. When they stood shirtless before each other, she opened them again.

Mollie was trembling as Roger again took her in his arms. Her nipples, already taut from the touch of his hands and mouth, now came into contact with the rough hair of his chest and suddenly, for both of them, their leisurely pace was too slow. With what seemed like one swift gesture, Roger shed the rest of his clothes and swooped Mollie, now equally naked, into his arms and onto the studio couch.

They made love swiftly, passionately, driven by a

desperate, suddenly overwhelming hunger, moving in a primal rhythm. Their bodies became one, responding to each other in perfect unison as they experienced a kaleidoscope of feeling. United intimately with Roger, Mollie freely expressed through the touch of her hand, the caress of her lips, all the pent up love and yearning she'd long denied. And miraculously, in giving of herself she began to feel that she had found herself, found the Mollie from whom she had long been estranged. She was part of him, and he was part of her in a togetherness that transcended their physical melding. Even after the final shuddering release that left them spent and trembling, Mollie continued to feel at home in Roger's arms. He cradled her so closely that the full length of her body touched every inch of his. . . . She was still inextricably connected to him.

She could think of no words to describe what she had experienced. As she lay there, filled with a great peace, Roger's warm breath tickled her ear. "Mollie, Mollie," he whispered. "My marvelous Mollie." Turning to face him, she thought she glimpsed in his eyes for a single moment what she had hoped to see—but it was gone before she could be sure.

For a time they lay together quietly. Then lazily, almost idly, Roger's hand began to roam across her back. "I think," he said throatily, "that we skipped a few steps back there. We got to know each other without being properly acquainted."

"Roger. . ." she began.

"Shh, shh. I must learn you—every curve and hollow of you." For a fleeting moment she resisted. "No, Mollie," he whispered. "No false shame between us. I won't accept anything less than all of you." And as he spoke, his hand traced a path of fire down her back, across her hips, and along her legs.

Taking Mollie's hand in his, he placed it firmly on the warm center of him, and she exulted to feel him spring to life at her touch. With an urgent gesture he guided her hand to imitate his own bold exploration— and oh, the splendor of his flesh, the delight and wonder of it!

Mollie had thought she was replete, but as Roger's hands and mouth, like delicate instruments, played slowly over her body, finding each of her secret places, she became filled with an indescribable languor, a sweetness she had never known before. Who was this man who could be so passionately urgent, so surprisingly tender? How could he know so well what she wanted— know it before she did herself? She felt as if she had come out of a dry desert into a lush countryside—and wondered if this happiness could really be hers.

But she couldn't think. Other forces were claiming her once again. She was enthralled by his unhurried, knowing movements. He, in turn, was filled with pleasure and pride in her response. Somewhere in the world a bell was tolling for someone. But within these four walls she and Roger were safe together, protected from pain, suffering, and death. All too soon the world would reclaim them, but *now...now...*. To Mollie's surprise she realized she had spoken the word out loud.

"Yes, my darling, now," Roger said, and slowly, slowly, he gathered her to him in the deepest, most satisfying embrace, bringing her with him to the brink of ecstasy and beyond...

Mollie had no idea how long she had slept when she was awakened by the sound of a child crying. She heard someone stirring on the other side of the wall, and then the soft murmur of a woman's voice crooning comfortingly. Jean-Pierre must have had a nightmare, but Madeleine was obviously at his side. No doubt all would soon be well.

Careful not to wake Roger, Mollie crept from the couch and slipped into her robe. She raised her hands to her neck, and ran her fingers languidly through her hair, letting the tumbled mass fall in soft disorder. She was ravenous, but Bjorn had stripped the cupboard clean. With a sigh she turned back to the couch. Roger was stirring restlessly, his hand searching the now vacant space beside him. The vulnerability of his nude, sleeping body touched her deeply.

As if aware of being watched, he opened his eyes and was immediately totally awake. "Why have you deserted me? Come back, woman. The night is still young."

Mollie sat down beside him, and immediately his hands slipped into the opening of her robe.

"It's almost morning," she said, nodding briefly toward the pale light behind her window as her hands automatically began tracing the contours of his angular face. She ran a single finger across the stubble of beard that covered his chin. "I got up because I heard a child crying."

"That was probably me you heard," he replied huskily. "Miserable because you had left me here alone, turning the bed into a frozen tundra." He raised himself on one elbow and added teasingly. "My mother always warned me that women would have no respect for me if I let them have their way."

"Idiot," she replied, bringing the flat of her hand down on his chest in a gentle push. "That *was* a child I heard."

"Yes, it probably was," he agreed with a groan that betrayed a hint of exasperation. "But what's that got to do with you?" He patted the place beside him. "Come back to bed, Mollie. After all," he added with a wicked gleam, "I'm not prone to argue."

"Always the author...and always the master," said Mollie, pulling a light blanket over them as she slipped alongside him with an exaggerated pantomime of obedience. On the other side of the wall everything was now quiet.

They lay together peacefully, Mollie cradled in

Roger's arms, luxuriating in the rightness of it.

"Would it sound too hopelessly unromantic if I confessed to being hungry?" he said after a few minutes.

"I thought you might be." Mollie laughed. "I'm feeling kind of peckish myself. That's another reason I got up—to make breakfast. But if you'll remember, your friend Bjorn has eaten me out of house and home."

Roger groaned theatrically. "Hell of a friend he is," he said in mock anger. "We'll have to go out. . . . What time do you think cafes in this neighborhood open?"

Mollie didn't know, and now that she was next to Roger again, her hunger had miraculously disappeared. She was content to lie next to him, both of them watching the window grow lighter and lighter. Finally, burrowing his face in her hair and tightening his hold on her, he said, "Well, if we can't eat, we might as well—" She stopped his mouth with a kiss.

"I always knew you were a quick learner," he retorted when she finally pulled away, recognizing her ploy as one of his own. "However, I like it." He sighed and dropped back against the pillow contentedly. He had closed his eyes again and Mollie found herself studying his features.

"What are you thinking?" she asked. Almost immediately she regretted the question.

He moaned. "I'm not thinking—or at least I'm trying not to. Not yet."

But an imp seemed to have gotten hold of Mollie's tongue. "Why are you trying not to?"

Now his eyes opened wide. "Because, as you yourself have just learned in the last few hours, thought is an impediment to desire. At the moment I'm not interested in generating a conflict of interests."

As though only now becoming aware of the chill morning air, Mollie drew the blanket more tightly around her. "Is that what you've decided I was feeling? Only desire?"

"I can see you're going to insist that I think when I'd much prefer not to." He placed his hands behind his head and stared stubbornly up at the ceiling. "How am I supposed to know what you were thinking or feeling?" he asked.

She tried to move away, but he drew her back beside him. Using her last bit of will power, she put her hand on his to arrest its movement. The man beside her, the man whose flesh warmed her skin, whose strong hand she held in hers, was the one she had waited for, the one she loved. But though she could read her own heart clearly, she could not be sure she had read his. And she had to know. He had spoken of desire, but not of love. The difference was crucial. For like him, she would accept nothing less than everything.

He allowed his hand to remain imprisoned in hers, but his lips roamed freely.

"You know," she said tremulously, "I'm not a Quaker, but I did go to a Friends school in Philadelphia. And one of the things I learned there was how important it was to 'heed the intimations within.'"

"That's exactly what I'm doing," he said huskily.

Her hand closed on a tangle of his thick dark hair, and she urged his face up to hers. Slowly, at his own pace, his lips moved hungrily up her body, pausing here and there seemingly at random, but somehow marking a path of pleasure.... It would have been easy, she realized, to forget everything she wanted to say, but she bit her lips in determination and only when their eyes were level did she release her hold on him.

"Roger," she said breathlessly, "this is important to me—to us, if there is to be an us. You said you wanted me to come to you freely. Well, I have. But now there's something I must know. What do the intimations within tell you?" she asked, returning to her earlier question.

"That you're warm and fragrant. That you're..."

"...above all, here," she finished sadly. "Look at

me, will you?" She was angry now. "I'm Mollie Paine,
I live and work in New York and—"

"I knew we'd met somewhere," he retorted dryly,
rising from the couch and beginning to dress.

Mollie could see he was fighting for control. Oh God,
she prayed silently, don't let him say something I can
never forgive!

"You know," he said, his manner once more aloof
and arrogant, "in our short but stormy history our dis-
cussions have always led to quarrels. Hasn't it struck you
that talk may be our problem rather than our solution?
Words lose their meaning once bodies touch."

Part of her felt that he was right. She wanted everything put into words, yet words seemed inevitably to lead
them to quarrels. On the way up to the studio she had
been so sure that what she was feeling was honest—and,
if necessary, enough for both of them. That she was in
touch with the intimations within had seemed enough.
His arms and lips had seemed enough. His strong, firm
body had seemed enough. Why had she begun asking
so many questions when questions always led to rifts
between them? "It is the little rift within the lute/That
by and by will make the music mute." Tennyson, she
thought inconsequentially, and laughed out loud.

Roger's face turned white with fury. "I don't see anything funny in the situation. If you think . . ."

A soft tap sounded at the door, and Mollie, who was
about to fling herself into his arms before he could say
anything irrevocable, drew away from him guiltily. "We
must be keeping Madeleine awake," she said, pulling on
her robe as she ran to the door.

Madeleine Renal stood in the hall, obviously deeply
distressed. Frantic, she clutched wildly at Mollie, who
felt her tremble.

"What's the matter, Madeleine?" Mollie asked soothingly, drawing her into the room.

"It's Jean-Pierre. He woke up a little while ago complaining of a stomach ache. At first I thought it was the apple tart I had made for dinner. I'm sure he ate more than was good for him." Nervously, she explained that she had given him some medicine, thinking it would help his indigestion, but he seemed worse now. When she had held him in her arms, he had screamed as she touched his side.

"Let me see him," Roger said, already halfway across the room.

"Ah, monsieur, I can't apologize enough for disturbing you at this hour, but—"

"No apologies are necessary, madame," he answered gently, without breaking his stride. "But let's not waste time."

He was the first one inside the sparsely furnished but immaculately clean apartment next door, followed by a still apologizing Madeleine, and Mollie. Little Jean-Pierre lay on his bed, moaning softly. Roger leaned over and murmured comforting words as he carefully probed the child's side with the tips of his fingers. The boy screamed.

"We have to get him to a hospital immediately," Roger told the child's mother.

"But how, monsieur?" She was becoming hysterical. "Shall I wake Monsieur Robinet and use his phone to call a doctor?"

"I'm afraid there's no time for that," Roger said, already lifting the boy from the bed and wrapping him snugly in a blanket. "Mollie, is there anyplace nearby where we can be sure to find a cab at this hour?"

She had already considered the possibilities. "Yes, of course. There are always a few cabs parked outside the restaurants at the Ecole Militaire metro stop. That cafe where we had breakfast—you remember?"

"Yes, I remember," he answered, giving her a tight smile. "That will have to do. Don't bother coming, Mollie. I'll handle it. We'd better hurry, Madame Renal."

"It hurts," moaned Jean-Pierre. "It hurts."

"Yes, I know it does," said Roger. With his usual effortless efficiency, he had cradled the little pain-wracked form in his arms and was moving toward the door, Madame Renal, who had stopped to grab a coat, on his heels.

As they disappeared down the steps, Roger's voice floated back to Mollie. "Don't worry, Jean-Pierre. It's all right to cry because you're only a little boy and I know it hurts. But I promise you'll feel better soon."

"Roger!" Mollie called after him.

But there was no answer.

- 9 -

ROGER WAS SURPRISED, almost disapproving. "Are you sure?" he asked. "Have you thought it through?"

Ignoring his question, she descended onto the sand. Above her towered the spire-topped monastery of Mont Saint-Michel. Far away, out of sight, she heard the sea. Then Odette appeared from nowhere. "It's the *grand marée* that sweeps all before it," she said. "But the treacherous sands are better than the smug safety of the solid rock. Only appetite is real. The rest is illusion." A great roaring came from behind Mollie. Terrified, she turned in time to see the tide roll in, sweeping over the sun-parched sands, rushing up to overwhelm her. The sight was beautiful but terrible to behold, and she covered her eyes with her hands. Just as she began to lose her footing and fall into the swirling water, strong arms lifted her to safety...

Mollie awoke abruptly and sat up, still trembling. The hours since Roger's departure had seemed endless. She had lain down fully clothed on the couch, her small transistor radio turned low and pressed against her ear. Voices and music came to her from various parts of Europe, from the entire world. She remembered thinking, as she fell into an exhausted sleep, that the sound waves were always in the air around her, yet she couldn't hear them without the radio.

A light tap on her door brought her fully to the present. Quickly switching off the radio, she rose and went to the door.

One look at Madeleine's face told her everything was all right. "I'm sorry to awaken you, Mollie, but I thought you'd want to know."

Ignoring her apologies, Mollie drew her into the room, glancing hopefully into the corridor as she closed the door. It was deserted. Roger hadn't returned with the young widow. "How is Jean-Pierre?"

"He's fine now," Madeleine assured her, sinking into the chair. "It was appendicitis, and the doctor said we didn't get him to the hospital a moment too soon." A shudder ran through her. "What would have happened to my poor boy if it hadn't been for Monsieur—for Roger?" Her smile was radiant as she added. "You should have seen him at the hospital. I-I'm afraid I went to pieces. I was so afraid. If I lost Jean-Pierre . . ." Her voice faded, then came back. "Anyway, Roger was wonderful. He seemed to know just what to do, and he stayed with me all the time."

Mollie could think of nothing to say, and after a moment Madeleine rose wearily from the chair and inspected the needlework she had done on it. "I see my little mending job has held."

But Mollie wasn't interested in the chair. "Didn't Roger come back with you?" she asked, hoping desperately despite the evidence to the contrary.

"No." Madeleine answered without turning around. "He must have been quite tired. We took a taxi back from the hospital, but he went on when we arrived here."

When Mollie remained silent, the other woman turned and studied her for a moment. "You know," she said slowly, with an emphasis that gave her words added significance, "sometimes a mended tear will outlast every inch of the fabric itself."

Mollie realized at once that her friend—and there was no doubt that Madeleine Renal was now a friend—had sensed the rift between her and Roger. With a sob she threw herself into the woman's outstretched arms.

"There, there," Madeleine said comfortingly. "It's going to be all right, I'm sure. Do you know," she added, laughing, "that the day before François and I agreed to marry we had a stupid quarrel? I thought I'd never see him again. *How* I cried! How I cried."

She waited until Mollie became quiet, then she said, "I must get some things for Jean-Pierre. The doctor said he would be coming down from the recovery room at about noon, and I want to be there when he does."

Madeleine's hand was on the door before Mollie could bring herself to ask, "What shall I do?"

The other woman turned and looked at her steadily. "Do you really want my advice?"

Mollie nodded.

"Keep busy. Wait—but don't *just* wait. If he loves you, he'll come back. If he doesn't, then it's just as well you find out now." Overcoming her evident exhaustion, she drew herself erect. "Meanwhile, don't ever forget that the world is rich in other things." Her voice was firm with conviction, and she didn't wait for a reply.

Alone once again, Mollie found herself thinking how she had misjudged the young widow. Because Madeleine Renal was gentle and soft-spoken, she had appeared weak and dependent. Because she had loved François and still grieved for him, she had seemed to be as consumed by his death as she had been by his life.

Now, with sudden clarity, Mollie realized how wrong she had been. No one who had managed to take care of herself and an infant son could be weak and dependent, and no one who could say "the world is rich in other things" had lost a sense of identity. How foolish she'd been to judge Madeleine on the basis of appearance.

If Roger were indeed gone from her life forever—
dear God, don't let that happen!—she too would grieve,
but she would not despair of life itself. Or at least she
would try not to. But like all good advice Madeleine's
would be hard to follow. Every time Mollie saw Roger
he brought to life a part of her that had been closed off
for years. He freed her to respond to him with mind,
body, and soul. He helped her to understand for the first
time what love could be. To come so close, to know
such joy, and then to find it wasn't shared by the man
who had truly awakened her. . . . Though it was unden-
iable that the world was rich in many things, they didn't
feed the heart—they merely passed the time. Last night
she had been in Roger's arms; the memory of it lingered
in her innermost being, and the sense of loss was bitter . . .

Mollie showered and dressed with more care than
usual, choosing a pale yellow shirtdress with long sleeves
that could be rolled up if it became warm during the day.
She tossed a colorful paisley shawl into her shoulder bag
in case it got cold. Practical Mollie, she thought dryly,
ready for anything except what was already happening
to her.

Studying herself in the mirror, she was satisfied to
see that she'd concealed the ravages of the night before
with a little makeup. How did men manage without pow-
der and paint, she wondered, preparing to leave. Or
didn't they feel things as deeply as women did?

Mollie walked downstairs to the lobby, where Monsieur Robinet was standing in front of his loge with a
small blue-gray envelope in his hand. "This *pneumatique*
just came for you, Mademoiselle Paine. I was about to
bring it up."

As she opened the envelope, Mollie once more mar-
veled at a system that allowed a letter written at one end
of the city to be delivered at the other end in only a few
hours. It was now 11 A.M., and this must have been

mailed when the post offices had first opened that morning.

Dear Mollie,
  I expect to be in funds as soon as the *Paris-Match* office opens. If you're not otherwise occupied, can we all meet for lunch at noon on the terrace of Fouquet's on the Champs?
                              Bjorn

We all? Was Bjorn with Annie Dumont? Or did he assume Roger had spent the night at her place and would still be there? That must be it. Roger could not have arrived back at his hotel before Bjorn had left.

As Mollie strode briskly along the wide, tree-lined avenue de la Bourdonnais and turned onto avenue Rapp, she mulled over in her mind what the result of such a meeting among the four of them would be. Crossing the Pont de l'Alma, she checked her watch, saw she was very early, and decided to go the long way—up the avenue Georges V to the top of the Champs-Elysées, then down the always crowded boulevard to Fouquet's.

Though it was still well before noon when she arrived, Bjorn was already there—alone. A small pile of saucers on the table indicated that he'd been there for some time, and that he'd been drinking.

"You're alone?" he questioned, raising his slightly flushed face to her. "I thought that when Roger didn't return to his room last night—"

"Where's Annie?" Mollie interjected.

Instead of answering, he pointed to his cognac glass. "Would you like one of these?" He mercifully asked no details about Roger. "They've done wonders for me," he added.

Mollie disagreed. Bjorn was unshaven, bleary-eyed, and as close to depressed as she imagined he could ever get.

"A little early in the day for me," she finally said, "but I could use some food. Nothing French," she added, thinking for some reason of Annie Dumont. "Do you suppose this elegant place could rustle up something as unexotic as a toasted English muffin and tea?" She sat down beside Bjorn, amused by her own request.

"Where's Annie?" Mollie repeated a few minutes later, breaking into the silence when her order arrived. To the waiter's quickly disguised surprise, she had also asked for a ham sandwich, which she now broke into two, casually shoving half toward Bjorn with the intention of getting some food into him before he drank any more. It lay alongside his Hasselblad before he took it up and began eating mechanically.

"I guess Annie's still with Pierre Midi," Bjorn said, "or maybe with his American twin. What's his name? Larry Lambert?"

Mollie wondered when Larry had joined them.

"I thought you didn't know Annie," Bjorn added as he bit into his sandwich.

"I didn't till yesterday. I met her for the first time yesterday evening."

"What do you think of her?"

"Do you really want to know?" Mollie asked, pushing the remainder of the sandwich toward him.

Bjorn's good humor was returning. Though his mouth was full of bread and ham, he managed to laugh. "Oh, I've got a pretty good idea, but tell me anyway."

"A piranha," said Mollie, suddenly convinced that Annie was with neither Pierre nor Larry but with Roger. She explained her theory of the two types of women in Roger's novels.

"And this particular piranha feeds on the literary celebrities of our day?" Bjorn asked, considering the idea as he chewed. "You may be right. But what's the difference if she loves me? And I know she does, even though she went off with the other two yesterday and may have spent the night with one of them."

Mollie stared at him in amazement. "Then what makes you sure she loves you? And doesn't it bother you? I mean, her going off with—"

"I know what you mean," Bjorn interrupted sharply. More quietly he added, "I can't answer your first question. She loves me, I know. It's not that I'm conceited, but things happen between a man and a woman that leave no doubt."

He seemed to be remembering something, and it was a while before he went on. "As for its bothering me, of course it does. But we don't choose who we love." He put his huge hand over hers and patted it kindly. "People can't be judged only by what they do when they're between the sheets, Mollie. It's been my experience that people do the really terrible things in life when they're out of bed and fully clothed."

Remembering some of her experiences in the publishing world, Mollie could think of no reason to disagree. "Come on," she said. "Let's get out of here. I need exercise and fresh air."

Somewhat sobered by the food, Bjorn rose wearily to his feet, extracted a crumpled wad of francs from his pocket, and handed a bill to the waiter, who had been hovering suspiciously near this unusually seedy-looking client. When the waiter still looked unhappy, Bjorn disentangled another note and shoved it at him. "That ought to do it, even at Fouquet's," he said as they reached the street. "Where to?"

On a sudden inspiration, Mollie, quickly running over a mental list of previously planned expeditions, suggested that they leave Paris and their problems behind and take the RER metro extension to Saint-Germain-en-Laye. Odette had told her about a pool there. Maybe they could rent suits and go for a swim. Bjorn agreed enthusiastically, and half an hour later they were strolling along a broad esplanade overlooking the Seine. The sky was

almost sapphire blue—quite unusual for that region—
and the rooftops and monuments of Paris, more than
twelve miles away, were etched sharply in the crystal-
clear air.

They stopped for a moment to read a brass plaque that
told them that the nearby château had once been the home
of Catherine de Medici, who had fled it after an astrologer
predicted she would meet her death "near Saint-Ger-
main." As she lay dying in faraway Blois, Catherine
asked her confessor his name. It was Julien de Saint-
Germain. The stars always win, Mollie thought. What
will be, will be.

Then Bjorn, who had been silent all this while, started
to talk, as though replying to something she had said
only a moment before.

It would be too convenient, the nature photographer
was saying, to be able to divide human beings, or even
just women, into piranhas and jellyfish. Not only were
there all the shadings in between, as Mollie had insisted
to Roger, but even the seeming extremes were related.
For example, the pliant jellyfish had a sting that under
the right circumstances could be as deadly as a piranha's
bite.

Seeing he had caught Mollie's attention, Bjorn went
on to draw further examples from natural history. Mollie,
fascinated, forgot her own problems and listened intently
as they walked. "Does Annie share your interest in these
things?" she asked at one point.

Bjorn had been in a full flight of oratory, but he
stopped and said with a self-deflating laugh, "A woman
doesn't have to share my interests, only some of my
passions."

Something in his tone told Mollie he had taught himself to accept this without quite believing it. On an impulse and without knowing why, she stopped, stood on
tiptoes, and planted a kiss on his stubby jaw. Bjorn

looked surprised—but no more so than the couple who had just emerged from one of the nearby shrubbery-lined paths that led at intervals onto the broad esplanade. Roger and Annie!

My prophetic heart, Mollie thought to herself. She had somehow known Roger would be with Annie. And there she was, as tiny as Mollie remembered her, but vibrant in a scarlet silk sheath and the stiletto-heeled black shoes she'd worn the previous evening.

Their heads had been together and they'd apparently been deep in conversation. But at the sight of Bjorn and Mollie they stopped dead in their tracks. Annie started to turn away, but Roger gripped her elbow and forced her to come forward with him.

"I can't seem to turn a corner," he said, coming up to them, "without finding you two locked in an embrace." His eyes rested on Mollie with an insolent ease that made it clear he was not at all perturbed by the sight of them.

Bjorn looked briefly at Roger and shrugged, as if the remark deserved no comment. "Hello, Annie," he said simply.

"Ah! I was sure you two would turn out to know each other," Roger said with satisfaction.

"I can't say I knew the same about *you* two," Bjorn replied reproachfully. "It never occurred to me that you and Annie were . . . acquainted. She never talked about you, only about your books, and then only to say that though she admired them, she was also irritated by them."

Annie shot Bjorn a murderous look which did not escape Roger, Mollie quickly noticed. "Were you?" he asked, fixing a cold smile on the Frenchwoman.

The situation was a little like watching a hawk preparing to pounce on a robin redbreast, Mollie thought, but she had to admit to taking some pleasure in the scene. Besides, the redbreast had some powerful defenses . . .

"Was I what?" Annie replied sharply, obviously annoyed at being caught out. She had not returned Bjorn's greeting and had acknowledged Mollie with only the barest of nods.

"Irritated. By my novels, I mean." Clearly he was neither surprised nor angry to find that Annie's previous enthusiasm for his work had been designed merely to flatter him. He was, however, intent on making her own up to the lie. "Come on," he insisted, "be honest. Mollie's shown considerably more courage in risking an author's ire—though I do think she might have finished the manuscript before jumping to conclusions." He glanced swiftly at Mollie, then turned back to Annie. "What *do* you think of how the women in my books behave?"

"Their behavior is unimportant," Annie began glibly. "Action is merely material, and only thought is spiritual in essence." Annie herself looked bewildered by what she'd just said. Bjorn emitted a hoot of laughter, but was quickly silenced by Annie's gorgon glance.

"That's gobbledygook in the best French critical tradition, Annie," Roger said impatiently. "Be honest for once."

"Honest!" snarled Annie, finally giving frank rein to her temper. "Even your precious Mollie will learn soon enough that honesty isn't something men admire in women. As they get older, women behave exactly as men expect them to."

Her eyes flashed fire and her body grew as tense as a cornered animal's. "I've never known a man who wants anything but approval from a woman," she concluded angrily. "Or who looks into a woman's eyes hoping to see anything but his own reflection."

"Magnificent, isn't she?" said Bjorn, turning enthusiastically to Roger. "I've never seen better even in the jungles of Africa. A regular hellcat."

Mollie risked a sideways glance at Roger to see how he was reacting to his friend's spirited comment.

"A hellcat?" Roger questioned, weighing his words carefully. "So *I* thought too, but I see I've underestimated her." His features relaxed into a grin that surprised Mollie. "But don't worry, Bjorn. Once she calms down, she'll make a splendid hellcat."

"Yes, won't she," said Bjorn, laughing appreciatively when he realized what Roger was saying.

Annie glanced from one to the other, as though making up her mind about something. "Ve-r-r-y funny," she finally drawled, turning to Roger. "And now, if the literary quiz is over, I've a few more important things to discuss with Bjorn." Dismissing Roger, she fixed incredibly wide and innocent eyes on the big Swede. "It's about last night," she began.

"I'd rather you didn't go into the details," Bjorn said, looking uncomfortable and shooting an apprehensive glance at Roger.

"Oh, Bjorn, you *are* a fool," Annie said in a caressing voice that seemed to contradict her words. She linked her arm in his, and as they turned toward the path she had just come down with Roger, Mollie heard her say in a tone full of restored good humor, "Now, as I was saying about last night. It was simply that..."

Mollie and Roger watched them vanish, then turned to each other. He spoke first. "So she *was* the lady of the keys. I suspected as much when she sent me off for cigarettes so abruptly. Why didn't you say something?"

"Because it wasn't any of my business," Mollie said defensively. To herself she added, And I still hoped it wasn't any of yours.

But now? Now she wasn't sure. All she knew was that Roger had obviously gone elsewhere this morning for comfort or consolation or whatever else he needed after those long hours in the hospital. She had been right to fear that their lovemaking hadn't meant as much to him as it had to her. The proof was that he'd gone to Annie.

"She's gone off and left you," Mollie added inconsequentially.

"That's the wrong way of looking at it," Roger objected. "She's left *us* alone."

"I stand corrected once more," Mollie replied, acknowledging his greater precision with a mock bow. "But we seem to have switched roles."

He raised a quizzical eyebrow and waited for her to explain.

"It's just that editorial changes should really be my province. After all, you've supplied the plot, the setting, and a good number of characters." She thought again of Annie. "Some of the motivation should be left to me."

"Now you're being more than a little unfair," he said hotly, and it was Mollie's turn to look puzzled. "The setting," he continued, "was your idea, though I see no reason to complain. Paris is just about the perfect backdrop for any kind of story—espionage, politics, or even modern love."

Before she could respond, he rushed on. "As for the characters, you'll have to take responsibility for introducing as many as I did." She tried to protest, but once more he gave her no opportunity. "For Odette I am eternally grateful. While she might have entered the scene at a more opportune moment," he said with a smile, "all in all I don't think I would be willing to do without her. She has enlarged my conception of Woman. I'm already planning a novel in which she plays an important role."

"I suppose we're most of us just so much grist for the mill," Mollie replied, more bitterly than she had intended.

"Come now, Mollie," Roger answered with surprising good humor. "That's not at all like you. You've been neither seduced nor"—he hesitated—"abandoned. Two adults who knew what they wanted agreed to spend a happy interlude together. It was certainly an extraordinary one for me, Mollie, and I venture to remind you that it wasn't disagreeable to you, either."

A happy interlude . . . yes, she'd been afraid of just that. But he gave her no time to reply, returning without pause to the previous topic as if the interruption had been of only the most minor importance.

"As for Larry Lambert," he said, "I could easily have done without him. In fact, I might have reached the end of what I hope will be a distinguished literary career without ever running into him—unless, of course, the Modern Language Association put us on a single program under the mistaken impression that we're both representative American authors."

She had to laugh.

"There's that lovely sound," he said. "I was beginning to think I'd never hear it again." He took her hand in his as casually as though their quarrel last night had never happened, and they walked along the esplanade, indifferent to everyone but each other. In the distance Mollie could easily pick out the Sacré Coeur, the Arc de Triomphe, Notre Dame, and the Eiffel Tower, the latter rising proudly from the patch of green that was the Champ-de-Mars.

Suddenly she turned to Roger, her palm outstretched. "Pay up," she said curtly.

"Another penny?"

She shook her head. "No. I'm afraid I want much more this time."

"You always do, don't you?" he said wryly, his dark eyes gleaming with ironic amusement. "Well," he began slowly, feeling his way cautiously, "I'm not a wealthy man, but if you are temporarily embarrassed . . ."

"Not to worry," Mollie replied. "I have no intention of putting a serious drain on your royalties. At the moment all I want is one franc." She pointed to a telescope mounted on a parapet. An engraved stone provided a schematic map of Paris, enabling the viewer to choose the proper position for a closer view of one of the city's marvels.

"If it's no more than that..." He dropped a coin into the apparatus and a motor began to whirl. "What are you looking for?"

"That patch of green at the base of the Eiffel Tower. I want to see if couples still dance there as they did of yore."

"But that was little more than twenty-four hours ago," he protested.

"You're being too literal," she answered, turning away from the telescope. "I expected more sensitivity from you."

"Meaning?"

"Meaning that time should never be measured by the clock alone. Oh, that's good enough for the workaday nine-to-five world. But you and I know that real time is measured by the number and importance of the events it contains."

His eyes searched her questioningly.

"For instance," she continued, "I feel light years away from the woman who danced on that grass in her stock-inged feet, from the woman who escaped making a fool of herself that night only to do the job more thoroughly the following night." Despite her effort to speak lightly, she couldn't help the tremor in her voice.

"Mollie," he said gently, placing his fingers on her mouth just as the motor on the telescope stopped running. "Don't. You're a beautiful and intelligent woman, but as a philosopher you lack a certain objectivity."

"Really?" she said with a self-mocking laugh. "I rather thought I was doing quite well for an amateur."

Roger started to say something, then changed his mind, and they continued to walk in silence until they passed the little brass plaque telling the story of Catherine de

Medici's fruitless attempt to escape her destiny. "Que sera, sera," Mollie commented with an assumed lightness as she pointed it out to him.

Leaving the esplanade, they turned into the town. Roger led her through streets different from those she had walked with Bjorn earlier. At one point they passed a sign indicating the direction to the indoor pool. "I was looking forward to a swim," Mollie said, explaining to Roger that she and Bjorn had planned to take a dip before heading back to Paris.

"Never let it be said that a Herrick stood between a lady and her desires," was Roger's immediate response. He refused to listen to her protests, and within minutes they had found the place, rented suits and towels, and were standing in separate lines waiting to use the locker rooms.

"Let's meet at the deep end of the pool," Roger said. "And don't waste time trying to turn that tank suit into something from the Faubourg Saint-Honoré."

"I wish I could!" Mollie wailed with comic exaggeration. "I'm going to look like hell in it! Not only is it that awful penitentiary gray, but they didn't have my size. It's going to be way too small for me."

"Fortunately you don't have to parade before a panel of judges, Miss New York. Besides, the contest has been rigged and the only judge who counts is known to be highly prejudiced in your favor."

Before she could say anything more he disappeared, calling out over his shoulder, "You have just five minutes."

But when she appeared at the deep end little more than five minutes later, he was nowhere in sight. Self-conscious about standing around in her snugly fitting suit, Mollie decided to walk around the vast pool. She had just begun her promenade when she heard an "Oh" of admiration from behind her. She turned just in time to see Roger execute a perfect dive from the high diving board and smoothly enter the water. A moment later he surfaced, swam over to her, and lifted himself effortlessly over the side of the pool.

"This sure beats the old swimming hole," he commented, water streaming down his face.

The midafternoon sun poured in through the glass walls of the pool room, bathing everything in a warm amber light. "Silver in the moonlight, golden in the sun," he said, passing his hand lightly over Mollie's hair.

The gesture had not been a sensual one, Mollie knew, but she couldn't control the slight shock of awareness that went through her from the top of her head to her toes. Had he felt it too? Almost unconsciously her eyes traveled quickly down his lean, hard body. Clearly he had.

His dark eyes gleamed with awakened desire as they raked her body, coming to rest on her breasts, taut against the thin fabric of the too-small suit. "In my youth, cold showers helped," he said, his voice gruff and mocking. "Let's see if a pool will do as well."

Without waiting for an answer, he shallow dived from the edge of the pool. Mollie followed, and they spent a blissful half hour, forgetting everything but the pleasure of the moment as they swam easily and happily alongside each other. Although Mollie was a fairly good swimmer herself, she was no match for Roger. But after that first spectacular dive—was the peacock spreading his wings?— he suited his pace to hers, and both of them reveled in a sense of physical well-being.

Life *could* be beautiful, Mollie told herself as she returned to the locker room to dress. If only she could hold on to the pleasure she had just known. If only . . .

Roger was already waiting for her outside, though she had raced into her clothes and barely taken time to comb her wet hair.

"Feel better?" he asked.

She didn't pretend not to understand him. She *did* feel

better, but once again the imp of perversity seized her tongue. "Roger, I have to admit I loved every minute of it—tank suit and all—but now it's over, and it really hasn't changed much, has it?"

"What do you mean?" he asked, the smile fading from his face.

"Well, it hasn't changed how you feel about last night, has it?"

"Why should it? I feel about you now exactly as I did then."

Her mind caught at the ambiguity in his words, but she continued stubbornly. "Yes, of course you would. But I'm not equipped to handle this situation," she said, choosing her words with care. "I wonder how Annie would."

"Oh," he said impatiently, "what does it matter? Annie never makes a move without calculating the consequences, but that's Bjorn's problem, not mine."

"In other words," Mollie blurted out, "now that you know how she really feels about your books she's lost you."

Roger turned and looked down at her wonderingly. "But she's never had me," he said after a moment. "Do you think that I, of all people, don't recognize a piranha when I see one?" His tone was one of amazed disbelief, and his hand went to her cheek and gently stroked it. "What on earth have you been thinking?"

His words confused her just as his touch aroused her. "I'm sorry," she began. "I had no right to say that. But I thought you and..."

"You've read too many bad novels, Mollie—probably those sensitive ones Jim Lorne thinks you're so fond of." As they walked toward the station, he explained, "I got in touch with Annie to get back my manuscript. I wanted to do some more work on it—change the end, in particular. I should have called you, I know, but I was still digesting what had happened last night. There had been much for me to think about. I didn't even try to go to bed. I needed some fresh air, and Annie suggested we come out here."

Mollie could think of nothing to say. "You know, Mollie," he went on, "it's not just the other woman or the other man that interferes with love."

Mollie waited for him to continue. After a moment he merely said, "I suppose Madeleine told you that Jean-Pierre is going to be all right?"

But Mollie was not to be deflected from the subject of love. She had realized all along that to some extent she had reacted to Roger out of jealousy of "the other woman." Jealousy was clearly her besetting sin, although until she'd met Roger she'd never suspected it.

"Let me say what's on my mind, Roger. After last night it's important that I try to explain, that I be open—"

"Haven't you been up to now?" he asked sharply.

"Yes, as far as I went, but..."

He let go of her hand, stepped back, and looked at her with an unreadable expression. "In other words we both go back to our corners and come out swinging? Have I got you right?"

A wave of hopelessness washed over her. She thought again of last night. She would never regret what she had done, but she couldn't bear the idea of being picked up and dropped at will—and if he didn't really love her, if it was only sex for him, then sooner or later he would leave her, if not for Annie then for someone else. Mollie shook her head slowly. "No. I no longer want to fight. I surrender."

A glint of satisfaction shone in his eyes as he put both hands on her shoulders. "Let's not have any more misunderstandings, Mollie," he said urgently. "Just what do you mean by surrender?"

She removed his hands. "I mean," she said, forcing herself to speak precisely, "that I'm going back home.

Coming here was a mistake. My work is in New York, so that's where my life is."

"That's a very dull philosophy," he said in an even voice that gave no hint as to what he was thinking. "It leaves out so many other things."

"Not necessarily," she answered. "In any case, it doesn't leave out hope."

"Hope of what?"

"I don't know. I'm no longer sure what I hope for. But I suspect that last night I acted out of hopelessness, not hope." She forced herself to meet his eyes. "I wanted you more than I wanted my own good opinion of myself, and I was ready to become a jellyfish, like your Jenny. With everything between us still unsettled and unstated, I was willing to accept pleasure alone. I thought I was brave enough."

"And you're not?"

A man only looks into a woman's eyes to see his own reflection, Annie had said in a burst of anger. For once she had not been performing. But what does a woman hope to see when she looks into a man's eyes, Mollie wondered. She could not see clearly into Roger's, which were now fixed on her with burning intensity.

"I'm brave enough for some things," she replied, "but not for pleasure without love. It doesn't seem fair, but I evidently need both," she concluded. "Apparently men don't. They see love as a surrender of control. Women experience it as a fulfillment, an extension of themselves."

Roger listened in pitiless silence. "That's quite a little lecture," he said finally. "I suppose you'll try to tell me it's based on extensive experiences in these matters?" His eyes voice was sardonic, challenging.

"Well," she replied quickly, "I have, as you pointed out, read a number of novels on the topic."

They met each other's eyes and immediately began to laugh. By this time they had reached the metro station.

Mollie held out her hand in a gesture of farewell. "I think we ought to say goodbye while we're still both laughing," she said with utter seriousness.

Roger took her extended hand in both of his, and she willed her fingers to stop trembling. He smiled briefly. "Won't you even let me see you home?"

"No, I'd rather you didn't," she replied. "I've got a lot to do and a lot to think about. I need time to myself."

"Then I insist on seeing you tonight." Before she could answer, he placed a finger across her lips. "Don't say no. As a matter of fact, don't say anything. I'll pick you up at seven."

Mollie considered for a moment, nodded silently, and walked away, turning once to see that Roger was still looking after her.

The familiar scent of heliotrope came from a mauve envelope under her door. Odette! Mollie had quite forgotten about her friend since she and Roger had put Odette into the old-fashioned cab driven by the mysterious Sergei. Mollie picked up the letter and began to read:

Chère Mollie,

You have brought me luck. I am going to have an opportunity to improve my faulty Russian. Sergei is old but he now owns the taxi—also old but also still serviceable—which he drives since arriving here in 1920. We are leaving on a gastronomic tour of France. What a beautiful dream come true!

And just when my life was in such disorder . . . but then there is hope in disorder and one should never despair of life.

Odette

So much for Odette. At least Mollie's coming here had brought *her* luck.

The letter still in her hand, Mollie sank into the director's chair. Through the thin walls, she heard a radio playing softly. Madeleine must be back from the hospital. Mollie decided to stop in and speak to her later, but first she must arrange for a flight back to New York—an afternoon plane tomorrow or the day after.

Would Jim Lorne be glad to see her back early? She supposed that depended on what Roger did with the *A Woman in Love* manuscript. A lot had happened in three days. It was a pity, as he had pointed out, that she'd never had a chance to finish reading the manuscript.

With a sigh she pulled out a suitcase and began packing. A line from Odette's letter kept going through her mind like the refrain of an old song: one should never despair of life.

- *10* -

HIS INSTRUMENT STILL slung behind his back bandolier-fashion, the musician introduced himself as the Devil's Envoy, assigned to travel the world and sing about hapless lovers who, having failed to read into their own hearts, were claimed by Satan as his own. The diners laughed knowingly and hastily set down their forks and knives. In rapt silence they listened to haunting ballads of ill-starred couples swirled like autumn leaves in the winds of passion. Last of all, the musician sang a legend about a faithless sailor who was miraculously saved from a shipwreck, only to be drowned on his return by his mistress's tears.

The song reminded Mollie of her dream about Mont Saint-Michel and of the strong arms that had saved her from the raging waters. As the final chords of the musician's guitar died away and a clatter of applause broke out, Mollie remembered that she had awakened too soon to see her rescuer's face.

"You've been far away," Roger said, his voice low-pitched and intense. Before he could continue, the musician came to their table with a little tray already piled high with coins. Roger contributed generously. "You didn't happen to notice whether he had a cloven foot did you?" he asked Mollie when the man had moved on. "I have a sneaking suspicion he's not an envoy but the devil himself."

"What makes you think so?" Mollie asked.

Roger looked at her intently. "Perhaps because of this." He touched a corner of her eye to wipe away a drop of moisture.

"Just a few sentimental tears." Mollie laughed uneasily. "All in all, they do a woman good. It's a pity tears are so frowned on these days." She brushed the backs of her hands against her eyes. "There, you're quite safe from drowning now."

"Am I a faithless lover, then?"

Mollie only smiled in reply, and then to change the subject said with a forced cheerfulness, "Tell me how you discovered this marvelous place."

They were sitting in a small restaurant on rue Montagne Sainte-Geneviève, a hilly street that wound through the heart of the Latin Quarter. Roger hadn't told her where they were going, and Mollie was glad she'd decided to wear a simple black cotton scoop-necked blouse and an Indian print skirt. Anything more elegant would have been out of place among the casually dressed crowd packed into this hundred-year-old hostelry.

The meal had been simple but excellent. "Not *haute cuisine*," Roger had explained, "but a kind of *haute* peasant." Mollie was sure that even Odette would have approved of the flavorful pot-au-feu. But more interesting than the food had been the many talented amateur entertainers, students for the most part, who were literally singing for their suppers by passing the hat.

"I was here once with Bjorn," Roger replied. "The food's good, the entertainment's even better, and I like the atmosphere—though it tends to get a little rowdy as the night wears on."

"It's a lovely way to say goodbye to Paris," said Mollie. "Thank you for taking me here." And then, since he seemed about to say something about her imminent departure, she added hurriedly, "Are the entertainers all musicians?"

"Hardly," Roger answered with a laugh. "Bjorn told me he once paid for his meal by doing a turn of Swedish folk songs. Though he has many talents, I'm sure singing isn't among them. Not bloody likely."

They laughed at the perfect imitation. "You're probably right," Mollie said, "but still, I'm sorry to have missed that. By the way, where is Bjorn?"

"With Annie. I left them together at Saint-Germain-en-Laye. Apparently she explained everything—not that he questioned her too closely."

Mollie remained silent and waited for Roger to continue.

"When Bjorn caught up with Annie and Pierre Midi last night, she was pleased to see him, especially as he was a great help in keeping Pierre from sinking under the sorrow of his sudden wealth. Then they ran into Larry Lambert at the Forum, and Annie's enthusiasm about bringing the French and American muses together was too much for him. He took off in a huff while Pierre and Larry were working out English lyrics for 'L'Almighty Dollar.' "

"Poor Bjorn," Mollie said sympathetically.

"On the contrary. He's blissful. Annie seems sincerely in love with him, at least for the moment. Nothing can shake his conviction that they're meant for each other, and temporary rivals don't seem to bother him."

Mollie wasn't so sure about that. "Still," she began hesitantly, "when he realized that you and she knew each other—"

"Like you, he jumped to the wrong conclusions," Roger cut in. "Forget Bjorn. He's all right. Let's get back to important matters. For example, why have you given up on my book?"

"I never said I had," Mollie protested. "Whether I edit it or not is up to you. But whatever you decide, I'm going home."

"Then it's me you're giving up on." She made no

reply and after a moment he said, "It hasn't been all fun and games, our three days in Paris, has it?"

"That's exactly what it *has* been—fun and games." Her voice sounded too sharp even to her own ears, and she added quickly, "We did have fun together, Roger, and I don't regret any of it, not a single minute. There were times when I felt I'd never been so close to anyone before . . ."

"So you did too," Roger said softly.

Mollie waited for him to continue, but he remained silent. She reluctantly went on. "But I was wrong. Partly, it was the fun we had together that made me think . . ." Her voice faltered, then she recovered. "Unfortunately I was no good at the games part. I never understood the rules you were playing by."

Avoiding his eyes, Mollie began toying restlessly with her empty coffee cup, the gesture reminding her of their first lunch together at Pete's Tavern just a few weeks ago.

"And I thought that the fun we were having was only part of the game we were playing," said Roger.

Mollie raised her eyes from her cup and sat deathly still. "I don't understand," she said.

"No, of course you don't," Roger answered. "You were something new in my life and I wasn't quite able to accept it." He paused then added almost angrily, "Dammit! I wish you'd finished reading my manuscript!"

She looked at him blankly. What did that have to do with anything? "I meant to the night before we met in Jim's office, but he insisted I show Larry around town. . . . But in any case, I don't see the connection." As she spoke, she rose from her chair and stood staring angrily down at him. Was that it? Was she being punished because his author's vanity had been upset by an imagined slight?

Intent on their conversation, they had been unaware of what was going on around them, and now, as Mollie stood alongside the table, she was bewildered by a dozen voices clamoring, "A volunteer! A volunteer! That lovely lady has volunteered."

A group of eager young students swarmed around her and led her away. With no clear idea of what was going on, or what she had volunteered for, Mollie was momentarily frightened. Someone tied a handkerchief around her eyes and whirled her helplessly about in a kind of insane blind man's buff. She was gasping for breath when strong arms reached out to stop her mad progress around the room and hold her firmly. There was something strangely familiar about the situation, but it took her a minute or two to recognize it. The sensation of helplessness, the relief of rescue—it was like her dream about Mont Saint-Michel. Tearing the blindfold from her eyes, she looked up at Roger. The significance of her dream finally, belatedly, clicked into place.

"Don't panic," he murmured into her ear. "I told you it tends to get rowdy here as the evening wears on, but it's all in fun." They were surrounded by a group of good-natured but overexcited students. Now that her eyes were free and Roger was with her, Mollie was no longer worried. But she wondered how they could extricate themselves from the encircling crowd. She glanced toward the door just as, to her surprise, Larry Lambert and Pierre Midi entered. She was amused to see that Larry, after just a few days in France, had abandoned his designer clothes for an outfit that he might have bought in a Paris flea market. Before Mollie could react, Roger, who had also seen them, held up his hand to command silence.

His voice cut easily through all the tumult. "I'm afraid you've all misunderstood," he said. "My friend here got up to greet Pierre Midi, whom she had just seen come through the door." The crowd turned in the direction he indicated. "Of course, if you'd rather play children's games than hear this justly famous poet do his own rendition of 'L'Almighty Dollar,' that's up to you."

Confused shouts rose from the crowd. "But that would be a shame," Roger continued after a dramatic pause, "because Monsieur Midi has brought with him the American poet Larry Lambert, who recently completed an English version of this unbelievably popular song."

That did it. Oblivious of the insolence underlying Roger's words, the crowd abandoned him and Mollie and swept toward the newcomers.

"Such is the price of fame," Roger commented as he pressed some bills into the *patron*'s hand and led Mollie to the door. The wicked gleam in his eyes betrayed the fact that Mollie's rescue was not the only reason for his satisfaction.

Behind them the two poets, apparently somewhat dazed by wine and the boisterous jostling of the enthusiastic crowd, were still trying to understand what the people wanted. The Frenchman, who Mollie knew had recently had more than his share of idolization, acted blasé, but Larry, to whom international acclaim was still relatively new, looked frankly delighted. "They've gone bananas!" Mollie heard him shout happily as she and Roger finally reached the street.

She was still a bit bewildered by what had happened, and as they passed alongside the Pantheon and across Saint-Michel, she willingly let Roger lead her down streets she didn't recognize in the general direction of home.

"That wasn't fair to Larry," she said loyally.

"Think so?" Roger replied with devilish glee. "Seems to me the punishment fit the crime, but in any case he didn't appear to be all that unhappy about having fame thrust upon him."

Mollie couldn't help laughing, but her heart wasn't fully in it and she stopped short. The silence between them lengthened as every step they took brought them closer to her studio and their final farewell.

"I had given up hope of finding you," Roger said abruptly, his voice breaking into the quiet of the night, "and I was trying to make do by imagining you in my writing."

"In your writing?" Mollie's surprised tone conveyed her disbelief. As she had learned on several occasions, much to her sorrow, the ego of authors was overwhelming. If in spite of everything that had happened, in spite of everything she had said, he persisted in seeing her as part of a gallery of Amandas and Jennys, she was right to give up the struggle and go home. He would never understand her as she really was.

"A penny?" Roger said suddenly, ignoring her question.

"For my thoughts?" she answered nervously, and then echoed his own reply when she had made him a similar offer during that first lunch at Pete's Tavern. "Are you sure you want to risk it?"

Even as she spoke the words, she wondered if all this repetition was symbolic. As it began, so shall it end? It came as no surprise when he replied, "I can afford it— even on what I get from Jim Lorne."

Yes, he too was remembering. His choice of words was no coincidence.

"I'm not sure *I* can risk it," she eventually answered. If she told him what was on her mind, it was sure to lead to a quarrel, and she knew she had used up all her reserves of strength. It was another soft, balmy spring night, and they were at peace, even if only temporarily. Everything conspired to make Mollie accept the sweet melancholy of defeat, when she had no more hope of winning—and nothing left to lose. Tomorrow she would go home, and it wouldn't matter at what cost she had won this moment of tranquility.

But she couldn't pay the price. She had to risk an argument in order to ask him. "It's just that I don't understand what you meant," she said, "when you said a little while ago that you'd imagined me in your writing." She stopped walking and faced him. "Listen to me, Roger. For all I know, you mean to flatter me, but frankly I don't see much resemblance between myself and the women in your books."

Mollie expected a caustic reply, but Roger's only response was an ominous silence. He put his hands in his pockets and they began walking again.

"For one thing," she continued with a weak laugh, "thanks to their author they're considerably more articulate than I am. I'm obviously no good at explaining things, or you'd have understood before this what I've been trying to say. There's a limit to the price I'll pay for what I want, no matter how desperately I want it."

"Yes. I know that," he answered calmly.

Mollie whirled to face him once more. "Then how can you say—"

"Stop," he commanded.

Surprised, she did as she was told.

Without taking his hands out of his pockets, his eyes never leaving hers, he bent to kiss her. It was a long kiss, both tender and passionate.

"That one was for me—to give me courage," he said roughly.

"For what?" Mollie asked, wondering how this imperious, sublimely self-confident man could ever need more courage.

"Your articulate author is having a bit of trouble finding the right words," he replied. "You'll have to let me circle around a bit, Mollie. A lot's riding on this for me," he added cryptically.

"Go on. I'm listening."

They were passing a little church park, and without a word they turned in and sat down on one of the benches. "Back in the restaurant," Roger resumed, "you were surprised when I brought up the fact that you had never finished reading the manuscript of *A Woman in Love*."

Mollie interrupted. "I tried to explain that Jim Lorne unexpectedly stuck me with Larry and that I hadn't had time. You're obviously infuriated by the idea that anybody, having once started your precious book, could put it down. Well, if it's any consolation to you, I was sorry I had to."

She stopped to catch her breath before going on. "Yes, it made me unhappy, but that was probably because you were telling me something I don't really want to know, in spite of the fact that I recognized it as the truth. I admitted it. Your portraits of Jenny and Amanda are accurately observed. What I still won't admit is that—"

"Quiet, woman. Don't be constantly interrupting." He smiled to take the sting out of his words, and continued without missing a beat. "When I overheard your comment to Lorne about the book, I knew you hadn't read very much of it, and my first thought was pleasure at how foolish you'd feel when you found out that you were wrong—when you found out that I *could* conceive, and in fact *had* conceived, of a woman different in every way from my Jenny and my Amanda."

He paused, drew a deep breath, and went on. "Then we talked and went out to lunch and everything changed. I didn't want you to read the last part of the book."

"Why?" Mollie asked in a low voice.

"Because I realized I had fallen in love with you ten minutes—no, five minutes—after I met you."

"Roger!"

"And I couldn't bring myself to trust you," he continued inexorably. "Or myself. As I told you then, my experience has been only of Jenny and Amanda. I couldn't really believe that the woman of my dreams existed. And if you'd read the manuscript, you'd know what my dream was—"

"I don't understand," she interjected, still afraid to believe what she thought he was trying to tell her.

"Patience, Mollie, patience," he said impatiently, then laughed at his own contradiction.

"Ve-r-r-y funny," Mollie shot back, imitating Annie's exaggerated way with *r*s.

"I'm glad you approve," he replied with a trace of the old complacency. "Humor is one of my nicer qualities. There are other less admirable aspects that it may take you years to get accustomed to."

Mollie was stunned, but he gave her no time to speak. "No, let me finish. I made Lorne get the manuscript back from you and spent the next week in agony. I loved you. And in spite of what you may think, I do know the difference between love and lust. Love is by far the more frightening surrender.

"Anyway," he continued, "by the time you had been gone a week I knew I couldn't run away from this—or from you. I came over with the manuscript and was going to ask you to read it. Maybe then, I thought, you'd forgive me for my insufferable behavior toward you. I cringed every time I thought about it and hoped that if you read what I foolishly found so hard to say, I could make you change your mind about me and we could start fresh."

"But . . ."

"Yes indeed, *but*. But when I found Lambert in your room, I grabbed at the situation as proof that I had been wrong about you. After all, if you were just another dishonest, manipulating woman, I didn't have to risk making a fool of myself."

"How unfair! I couldn't have been more honest with you! I've never said a word to you that—"

"Don't rub it in, Mollie," he interrupted. "I'm not stupid, just obstinate. Don't you understand? The more you were you—the more you were everything I'd ever wanted—the harder I fought to escape. I tried to tell myself that if we could just have an affair I'd be able to get you out of my system. And then, after our argument this morning, I realized that wouldn't work, that you'd risked *your* vulnerability, and that I'd damn well have to chance mine. I could see," he said grimly, "that just as you'd had enough courage to come to me, you'd have enough to walk away." He held her face between his two hands. "I won't let you do that, Mollie."

"You were the dishonest one, Roger," she said slowly, disengaging herself. "I don't think I care for that." Despite her words, her heart was beginning to hope once again.

Knotting his hand into a fist, he pounded his chest three times. "Mea culpa, mea culpa, mea maxima culpa!" he cried. His look of genuine contrition was quickly spoiled by the tone of the remark that followed. "Aren't those the words a woman most wants to hear?"

"No!" Mollie replied hotly. "She'll generally, and often stupidly, settle for 'I love you.'"

"Haven't I already said that?" he asked, bewildered.

"Not *to* me, Roger. What you've said *to* me," she continued inexorably, "is everything but. You've been very careful never to let that statement pass your lips. Not even last night..."

"How careless of me!" They had risen from the bench and were once more walking, but now Roger stopped and gazed intently down at her. "I love you. *Je t'aime. Ti amo. Te quiero. Ich liebe dich.* I'll happily say it in every language I know, Mollie, but dammit, you're supposed to be one of the best editors in New York. You should have been able to read between the lines!"

What audacity, Mollie thought. But he looked so rueful that she softened immediately. He loved her! She still couldn't believe it, but she felt poised on the brink of an incredible happiness.

Roger returned to his story. "I'm not doing very well, am I?" he asked. "Let me get back to my novel. I should probably have started with *her* ... with my dream..."

Mollie waited in puzzled silence for him to proceed.

"She's introduced toward the end when Jason, my protagonist—I can hardly call him a hero—leaves Chicago to lick his wounds after the latest of his unhappy romantic entanglements. On the plane he meets a different sort of woman—lovely, attractive, challengingly highspirited. They begin to talk and soon become involved in a duel of wits."

Mollie listened attentively.

"Jason finds it difficult to accept her theory that the male-female relationship is not a struggle for dominance but part of a never ending dialogue by which the sexes reveal themselves to one another. Experience has taught him to be wary."

He turned and sought her eyes with his. "Try to understand, Mollie," he said urgently. "Please.... Though he is immensely attracted to her, he is unwilling to recognize his good fortune. In the three-hour flight from Chicago to New York they go through every stage of romance, including a final breakup, without even learning each other's names."

His voice was strained. "He loses sight of her at the airport, and as he gets into the taxi that is to take him into the city, he begins to think that he only imagined it all, that perhaps there was no such person on that plane with him . . ."

The last echoes of his voice had hardly faded before Mollie said, somewhat unsteadily, "As an editor, I can tell you your readers won't care for the inconclusive ending." In his eyes she saw again what she had glimpsed the night before. But now it was shining steadily. Gone was that "now you see him, now you don't" sensation that had haunted her. . . . He was really there for her, and he loved her.

"Damn the book! It's my life—*our* life—I'm talking about," Roger burst out impatiently and her spirit soared. "Anyhow, at the time the character was only someone I'd imagined." He took Mollie's hands in his. "I have a better grip on her now," he said, drawing her close. "You will give me time to work out a different ending, won't you, Mollie?" For the first time his voice was tinged with doubt. "She's a very complicated woman—wise and witty, beautiful and honest and sexy. I'll need years and years to study her at close range. Marry me, Mollie. Please say you will."

She turned her face up to his and found she couldn't speak. Nevertheless, her tear-filled eyes and brilliant smile told him everything.

His voice was throaty as he murmured, "Let's go back to that charming little place I always thought would be so fine for a loving two." They were within sight of the Eiffel Tower. Rue de Grenelle was only a few minutes away.

"Yes," she finally said in a happy rush. "Yes, my darling, of course I'll marry you." She placed her hands on his chest where his heart was beating as madly as her own. Her fingers slid upward to wrap around his neck and pull him to her until their lips met in a deep and tender kiss. "Yes," she repeated breathlessly, "yes, I will marry you, Roger. And yes, let's go home first, please, and be a loving two together."

He grinned back at her, happy and triumphant. Hand in hand, they ran through the streets of Paris, their pounding footsteps and exultant shouts drifting up to the star-filled sky.

Second Chance at Love™

WATCH FOR
6 NEW TITLES EVERY MONTH!

Second Chance at Love

WHAT READERS SAY ABOUT
SECOND CHANCE AT LOVE

"SECOND CHANCE AT LOVE is fantastic."
—*J. L., Greenville, South Carolina**

"SECOND CHANCE AT LOVE has all the romance of the big novels."
—*L. W., Oak Grove, Missouri**

"You deserve a standing ovation!"
—*S. C., Birch Run, Michigan**

"Thank you for putting out this type of story. Love and passion have no time limits. I look forward to more of these good books."
—*E. G., Huntsville, Alabama**

"Thank you for your excellent series of books. Our book stores receive their monthly selections between the second and third week of every month. Please believe me when I say they have a frantic female calling them every day until they get your books in."
—*C. Y., Sacramento, California**

"I have become addicted to the SECOND CHANCE AT LOVE books...You can be very proud of these books....I look forward to them each month."
—*D. A., Floral City, Florida**

"I have enjoyed every one of your SECOND CHANCE AT LOVE books. Reading them is like eating potato chips, once you start you just can't stop."
—*L. S., Kenosha, Wisconsin**

"I consider your SECOND CHANCE AT LOVE books the best on the market."
—*D. S., Redmond, Washington**

*Names and addresses available upon request